THORNE'S ROSE

SAVAGE HELL MC BOOK 8

K.L. RAMSEY

ROSE

Rose Savage walked into her cousin's bar knowing that she shouldn't have been there but daring to break all her father's rules. Her dad and Savage's father had a falling out years ago before Savage's father passed. Her dad had forbidden her to step even one toe into Savage Hell, but really, she had no choice. If she wanted to keep her little girl safe, she was going to have to face down the man her father swore was the devil himself.

"Can I help you?" a handsome man behind the bar asked.

"Um, I'm trying to find Savage," she said. "I need his help. Is he around?"

"Well, I guess that depends on who you are," the man challenged. Rose put her hands on her hips and flashed him her best smile. "That's not going to work, honey," he insisted. "I appreciate the pretty smile and all, but no one gets in to see Savage without my approval. So, what's your name, honey?" he asked.

"Rose," she breathed, giving up on her attempt to act sexy for the guy behind the bar. Apparently, he wasn't buying what she was selling. Hell, she hadn't sold anything since before Sadie was born, and that had been going on for two years now.

"Rose what?" the man asked. He was starting to sound a bit annoyed with her and she wondered what that was about.

"Rose Savage," she said. "I'm his cousin."

"I see," the man said. "Stay right here, Rose," he ordered, "and don't talk to any of the guys if you know what's good for you."

"What's that supposed to mean?" she shouted over the music, but the guy pretended not to hear her.

Within minutes, the handsome bartender reappeared holding hands with her cousin. At least, Rose thought that it was Savage. He had aged some and was bigger than she remembered him being ten years ago when she last saw him.

"Rose," he breathed. She nodded and Savage picked her up and spun her around. "This is my husband, Bowie," he said, introducing her to the handsome bartender. "I'll introduce you to our wife, Dallas, when she comes in. What are you doing here?" Savage asked.

Hearing that Savage was married to both a man and a woman didn't surprise her much. She had known that her cousin was bi for years. He shared that with her when she was a kid but told her not to tell anyone else. "I need your help," she breathed.

"Of course," Savage agreed, "it's so good to see you."

"Um, you too," she said. "It's been a long time. I'm sorry that I wasn't able to come sooner to visit."

"No, I get it," he said. "Your father has his rules, but why now? I mean, you're breaking his rules now, right?"

"Yes, but he really can't get mad at me anymore," she admitted. She hated having to tell him this part. It wasn't how anyone should find out. "My father passed away over a year ago," she said.

"I see," Savage breathed, "I'm so sorry, Rose. What from?" he asked.

"Heart attack," she whispered. "It was awful. I had just picked up Sadie from daycare and went home to make Dad dinner."

"Who's Sadie?" Savage asked.

Rose smiled, "She's my two-year-old daughter."

"Congratulations," Savage said. "Wow, you're a mom."

"I am," Rose said, "and that's why I need your help. My ex wants custody of her and he's a bad man. If he gets his hands on Sadie, he'll destroy her spirit, and I can't let that happen. He beat me and I know that if given the chance, he'll do the same to her."

"What are his chances of getting custody of her?" Bowie asked.

"Good," Rose whispered, "he's very wealthy and can pay lawyers and keep me in court for ages. I don't have that kind of money. If Sadie has to live with him, I don't know what I'll do."

3

"All right," Savage said, "of course, I'll help you. What's this guy do for a living?" he asked.

"That's just it," Rose said. "He's a car salesman and a bad one at that. While we were together, he didn't sell many cars. He'd tell me business was slow, but he always had cash on him—a lot of it. He drives high-end cars and lives in a mini-mansion. I'm betting that he has a side hustle and that it's not legal."

"I'll need the name of the car lot he works for," Savage said. "I have a few ideas, but this will take a bit of time. Do you and Sadie have someplace safe to go?" Savage asked.

"No, not really," she said. "Every time I try to find a new place, he shows up. It's almost like my ex is staying one step ahead of me all the time."

"We have a guy who can help," Bowie said. "But you'll have to do as he says. He's kind of a control freak, but he's good at keeping people safe. Will you let him help you?" What choice did she have? If she kept trying to run from her ex on her own, he'd eventually catch up to them and take Sadie from her. Rose couldn't let that happen, not after they had come this far.

"I'll accept his help," she breathed.

"Thank you," Savage said. "How about you go pick up your daughter and come back to our place for dinner? We can call Thorne and get everything set up. He'll meet you at our house and take you and Sadie someplace safe while Bowie and I investigate your ex."

"I don't know how I'll ever repay you for this," Rose admitted. "I'm so grateful that you will help me."

"I don't need payment, Rose. You and Sadie staying safe is payment enough. Thorne is a good guy and I'd trust him with my life. You'll be in good hands," Savage said.

"Word of warning," Bowie said, "he's a bit rough around the edges. He's all bark and no bite though. Just keep that in mind when you meet him tonight."

"Will do," she agreed. "I'll pick up Sadie from my friend's place and meet you back here in about an hour. Does that work?" Rose asked.

"Yep, and then we can head back to our house. I'll let Dallas know that we'll have two more for dinner," Savage said.

"I don't want to put you or your wife out," she said.

"Not at all," Bowie soothed. "We have a boatload of kids. Two more mouths to feed won't be a problem." She liked hearing that Savage had a family and kids. She had always thought about her cousin as a loner, but she liked seeing him this way—settled down and happy.

"I'm glad that you found happiness," Rose said to Savage. "I'm sorry that we weren't in each other's lives more."

"Well, we couldn't make our fathers get along. And although I tried, I couldn't make your father like me. We'll make up for lost time now, Rose," Savage assured. "You'll find your happiness too, honey, I promise." Rose nodded and turned to leave.

"I'll hold you to that promise, Savage," she whispered to herself on her way out of the bar. She just hoped that it was a promise that he'd be able to keep.

THORNE

VICTOR THORNE GOT THE CALL FROM SAVAGE THAT HE HAD A gig for him, and he wanted to tell his club's Prez, no, but he also knew that was something he just couldn't do. He had just worked a double shift and he was dog-tired.

Since going undercover to root out the trafficking rings in the area, he was burning the candle at both ends. When he joined the CIA, he had no clue how many hours a week he'd be working, and when they stuck him on undercover work, those hours doubled. He was the guy that Uncle Sam sent in when there was no one left to do the job. He barely had time to sleep anymore and that's what he had planned on doing for the next six hours until he had to show back up to work. He was so close to cracking the trafficking ring that he had been working for, he just needed a few more days and then, he'd have the evidence that he'd need to bring down the whole organization and put every scum bag that worked for it behind bars.

He had been doing undercover work for almost eight years now because his boss said that he had the look for it. He knew that his boss took one look at his full upper body tattoos and decided his fate. He was right, Thorne had the look and that was because he used to live that life. He used to be the criminal that he now played, and that gave him a leg up. He knew how the assholes who ran the trafficking rings thought and being able to get into their sick minds was a big part of what made him a damn good CIA agent.

His orders from Savage were that he was supposed to meet him and Bowie over at their house tonight at about six. He knew that turning down his Prez's invitation to come over would be a huge mistake, so he agreed to be there. Apparently, Savage had a family member in trouble, and his skills at hiding people away were needed.

Thorne took a quick shower and got dressed, pulling on a clean pair of jeans and a T-shirt. Hopefully, this thing for Savage wouldn't take too long, and then, he'd be able to catch a few hours of sleep before heading back to work in the morning.

He drove over to Savage's house and parked behind Bowie's pick-up. Savage walked out and met him on the front porch, which was never a good sign. It usually meant that he was going to have to talk to Thorne before they got inside and that usually involved some news that he wasn't going to like.

"Hey Savage," he called.

"Thanks for coming out on such short notice," Savage said. "We have a little bit of a situation."

"What kind of situation?" Thorne asked.

"My cousin, Rose, and her two-year-old daughter, Sadie, need to get away for a bit. Her ex is bad news, and she needs to lay low while Bowie and I look into his extracurricular business activities."

"What kind of business activities are we talking about?" Thorne asked.

"He's supposedly a car salesman, but according to my cousin, he'd made too much money for the number of cars that he's selling. Rose is betting that he's involved in an illegal side business, but we need time to figure it out."

"I'm guessing that will take a bit of time," Thorne said. "Should I plan on this being a long-term thing?"

"Possibly," Savage admitted, "is that going to be a problem?" Thorne wanted to tell Savage that it was going to be a huge problem, but he wouldn't dare. He'd just have to figure out how to juggle his crazy work schedule and help out Savage's cousin, at the same time.

"Not at all," Thorne lied, "I'd be happy to help."

"Great, because I need a place for her and her daughter tonight. She thinks that someone's following her and if that's the case, I can't let her stay here with my family. I won't put them at risk," Savage said. Thorne didn't blame the guy. He would have felt the same way if he had a family to protect, but he didn't.

"Of course," Thorne agreed. "How about I meet your

cousin and her kid and if they're comfortable with everything, I can get them into a safe house tonight?"

"That would be wonderful. I'd owe you one, Thorne," Savage said.

"No big deal," Thorne lied. He was sure that helping out Savage's cousin tonight would only lead to him getting no sleep.

Savage nodded, "Follow me," he said. Thorne did as ordered and followed Savage into the back of the house to the kitchen.

"Hey, Thorne," Bowie said. Dallas kissed his cheek and asked if he wanted some dinner, and he lied and said that he had already eaten. The sooner he could meet Rose and get her, and her kid settled, the sooner he could crawl into his bed and get some shut-eye.

Savage nodded to the petite woman in the corner holding a toddler. "That's my cousin, Rose, and her daughter, Sadie." He took a step toward Rose, and she backed further into the corner. "Rose this is Thorne. He's a friend and you can trust him." She looked at Savage as though he might have lost his mind and Thorne wanted to laugh. He knew what she saw when she looked at him. He was covered in tattoos and looked more like a criminal than someone who was there to save her.

"Good to meet you, Rose," Thorne said. He smiled and waved to the toddler, "You too, Sadie." The little girl smiled back at him and waved. Well, at least one of the women he was going to have to protect seemed to like him.

"You're going to protect us?" Rose asked.

"I am," Thorne said. "If that's okay with you both. I'm good at what I do, and I will have no problem keeping you both safe."

Savage stepped between them and turned to Rose. "Listen, I know Thorne's a bit rough around the edges," he said.

"Gee, thanks for that," Thorne muttered. Savage shot him back a look and turned back to face his cousin.

"We all are," Savage covered, "but, I'd trust Thorne with my life, and I know that he'll keep you and your daughter safe if you'll let him."

"I trust you, Savage," Rose said, "it's why I came to you in the first place. If you say that Thorne will help us, then I trust you. Sadie and I will go with him." She turned to face Thorne and pasted on her best smile. "Thank you for offering to help us."

"Of course," he agreed.

"You'll stay in touch?" Bowie asked Thorne.

"Yes," Thorne agreed, "as soon as I get them settled, I will check in with Savage. I'll keep you guys in the loop."

"Thanks, man," Savage said. "I don't know how I'll ever repay you for doing this for my family."

"I'm sure I'll come up with something," Thorne joked, slapping Savage on the shoulder. He turned back to Rose, "How soon can you be ready?" he asked.

"We're ready now," Rose said. "I just need to change Sadie and then, we can be ready to go with you." She walked past him, and he caught a whiff of her strawberry-scented shampoo and Thorne made a mental note to stop sniffing the pretty girl. If he was going to keep his promise to Savage, he would need to keep his head in the game—strawberry-scented shampoo or not.

ROSE

ROSE PEEKED BACK AT HER SLEEPING DAUGHTER AND SMILED. As soon as Savage helped her load in the car seat and put her belongings into Thorne's pick-up, they took off. She barely got to tell her cousin how much she appreciated his help or even tell him and his beautiful family goodbye. Savage insisted that none of that was necessary because they'd be seeing each other again very soon, but she didn't believe that. Her ex would make sure that she'd never see anyone she loved again, if he had his way, including Sadie.

Thorne was hard to decipher. He wasn't much of a talker and sitting next to him in complete silence made her uncomfortable. "So, you have a family?" she asked, trying to break the annoying silence. She was usually a talker and verbal diarrhea was her specialty. When things were too quiet, she usually tried to fill the gaps with chit-chat that had no rhyme or reason.

"No," Thorne breathed.

"Um, okay. Where are you taking us?" she asked. All Savage had told her was that his friend was going to take her and Sadie someplace safe, but nothing was really specified.

"Someplace safe," he said. Rose rolled her eyes and sighed.

"A little more detail might help here, Thorne," she grumbled. "I don't know you and I'm trying to figure you out."

"Well, don't," he said. "I'm not much for talking and there's nothing to figure out. I'm taking you and your kid someplace safe and then, I plan on getting some sleep. It's been a long fucking day."

Rose peeked into the backseat to make sure that Sadie was still sleeping. "First, my kid's name is Sadie and second, I'd prefer that you not cuss around her. She's a sponge and picks up on everything right now."

"Yeah, that probably won't happen. I don't have kids, so cussing isn't something that I have to worry about. I'll try to cut it out, but no promises," Thorne said. Geeze, this guy was a real asshole.

"I'd appreciate that," Rose huffed. She crossed her arms over her chest, pissed that she had gotten nowhere with the guy. The least he could do was tell her where they were heading.

Thorne sighed, "Tell me about your ex," he said.

"I thought that you said that you weren't much of a talker?" she reminded.

"I'm not making small talk, Rose. I need to know what kind of trouble you're in and what, or in this case, who I'm dealing with. You want me to keep you and your kid safe, right?" he asked.

"Sadie," she reminded.

"Okay—you want me to keep you and Sadie safe, right?" Rose looked him over and noticed the vein in his neck looked about ready to pop and she couldn't help but laugh.

"You really do hate talking, don't you?" she asked.

"Yeah," he grumbled.

"I can tell by that vein in your neck that I grate on your last nerve," she added.

"You're not wrong about that either," he admitted.

"Fine, it's good to know where I stand with you, Thorne," she said. Honestly, it hurt her feelings that he didn't like her. Thorne didn't even know her yet, but he had already decided that she was a bother. It didn't matter though. As long as he kept his promise to Savage and kept her and Sadie safe, that was all she really cared about.

"Can we just get to the part where you stop looking at my vein and psychoanalyzing me? Tell me about your ex," he repeated.

"Fine," she spat. "His name is Joseph Stern," she said. God, even saying his name out loud made her want to dry heave.

"You two married or just together?" Thorne asked.

"We never got married, thank God," she said, "but, he's Sadie's father. He's on her birth certificate and he's got the means to fight me in court for her and win." The thought of Joe getting his disgusting hands on her daughter made her physically ill. How she was ever with a man like him was still a mystery to her. She definitely had on rose-colored glasses the night she jumped into his bed. That was a mistake she'd never make again. Rose wasn't ever going to let another man hurt her.

"And let me guess—he wants custody?" Thorne asked.

"Right, and I can't let him win. He used to beat me. That's why I took Sadie and left him. I can't let him do the same to her," Rose said.

"No, you can't," he breathed. "I won't let him touch her." Hearing Thorne make her that promise gave her hope that her cousin hadn't just pawned her off onto some bodyguard who wouldn't give a shit about her or her daughter.

"Thank you for saying that Thorne," she said.

"No problem," he said. "When was the last time you saw your asshole ex?"

"Language," she chided, "and, I saw him about three days ago. That's when I decided to head to Huntsville and find Savage. Our fathers were brothers, and they didn't like each other very much. Savage and I were close as kids until our fathers finally quit talking to each other. I haven't seen him in years, but I had a gut feeling that he'd still help us if I showed up on his doorstep." Savage had always been that type of guy. He'd help anyone who needed a hand. He was the kindest guy she had ever known. Savage gave Rose hope that she'd be able to find someone like him someday, but so far, all she seemed to attract from the male population was losers and assholes.

"He's one of the best guys I know," Thorne agreed. "He said something about your ex selling cars."

"Yeah, he's a car salesman and a bad one at that. He's always got a wad of cash on him though."

"So, you think that he's up to no good," Thorne concluded.

"Yeah," she agreed, "how else could he make so much money while not selling any cars?" Rose asked.

"Savage will get to the bottom of it," Thorne promised. "If he's using the car sales gig as a cover, he and Bowie will find out and tear him down. You won't have to do a thing except follow my orders so that I can keep you and our kid safe until they are done with your ex."

She sighed again. "Sadie," she breathed. Rose had a feeling that Thorne was just trying to push her buttons by calling Sadie a kid and cursing all the time. Maybe she should just let it go and then, he might stop, but she knew that guys like Thorne would just find another way to annoy her. It's how they seemed to work. Guys like Thorne were trouble and if she had learned anything from being with Joe, it was to avoid trouble at all costs.

💀 💀 💀

Rose woke up just as the sun was peeking over the horizon. "It's morning?" she asked.

"Yep, you fell asleep just after midnight," Thorne said.

"We've been driving this whole time?" she asked. How did she not wake up once during the night? She usually was up half a dozen times to check on Sadie, but last night, she slept like the dead.

"Yeah, well, except when I stopped for gas and coffee a couple of times," he said. "We'll be at the safehouse in about an hour."

"Where are we?" she asked. Rose fished around her purse for her cellphone, trying to find out what time it was, but she couldn't find it. "I think I lost my phone," she said.

"You didn't lose it. I took it."

"You did what?" she shouted, waking Sadie. The toddler cried out and Rose turned to soothe her. "You're all right, honey. We're almost there." Rose turned back to Thorne and looked him over. He didn't seem to be fazed by her anger at all. "Where is my phone?" she asked.

"I tossed it out the window about two states back," he said.

"You did what?" she whispered, trying to keep her daughter calm.

"You said that your ex caught up with you about three days before you found Savage. I'm betting that he's been tracking you by your phone this whole time." Well, that made sense since her ex held the contract on her cell phone. Rose had never gotten around to getting her own plan once she left him.

"Shit," she mumbled.

"Language," Thorne chided.

Rose rolled her eyes at him. "I never thought about being on his plan and him being able to track us. Thank you for getting rid of my phone, but I'll need a new one. Can we stop somewhere?"

Thorne dug into his jeans pocket and pulled out a phone.

"You can use this one. It's a burner and only Savage, Bowie, and I have the number. Don't call anyone else with it—especially not your ex."

"I have nothing to say to him, so that won't be a problem. Thank you," she said. "How much do I owe you?"

"Nothing," Thorne said. "Savage gave it to me to give to you when we got on the road. It's a gift from him."

"Well, I'll thank him the next time we talk," she said.

"As for where we are—you're in Texas," he said. "My home state."

"You're from Texas?" she asked. "I just assumed that you were from Huntsville."

"No," he said. "Most of the guys in Savage Hell are from another state. Hell, we just patched in a kid from California. A lot of the guys are military or retired and well, we just kind of stuck around Huntsville and found our home at Savage Hell."

"I take it you're military then?" Rose asked.

"Yep, I was in the Army until about two years ago, when I retired," he admitted.

"You retired two years ago?" she asked. "How old are you?" She knew that he must be older, just from the gray in his beard, but she never thought to ask. Plus, she was always told that it was rude to ask a person's age—well unless she was waiting tables and carding minors who were trying to sneak a drink at the bar.

"I just turned forty," he said. Thorne sounded a little put off by her question, making her feel bad.

"Sorry, I didn't mean to upset you. Forty isn't that bad," she said.

"Forty sucks," he said, "but I hear that the alternative is worse."

"What's the alternative?" she asked.

"Death," he breathed. "I'm good with being forty. Hell, I never thought that I'd make it to thirty, so I'm glad to be here."

"Well, I just turned twenty-five, and having a two-year-old, some days I feel like I'm forty," she joked.

"You're still a baby yourself," he said. "You were only twenty-two when you got pregnant?" he asked.

"Yeah, I was just a kid, practically. At least, that's how I felt. I didn't have any clue how to be a mom, since my own mother died when I was only seven. But I quickly figured it out. Plus, Sadie was a pretty easy baby. That's what my father used to tell me, anyway." She always felt sad when she talked about her father. Sure, he kept her from the only other family she had over a silly feud, but she still loved her father.

She was with him when he passed. She had just run to get Sadie from daycare, after working the day shift at the diner, waiting tables. She was exhausted, mainly from looking over her shoulder all the time, trying to see if Joe was following her. Rose took her daughter home and started making dinner for her father and her when she heard a thud from the other room. She turned off the stove and ran into the room to find her father lying on the floor. He was already gone by the time she had found him. Rose called 911, but she knew that it was a frugal attempt to save him, he was gone. She was just thankful that her daughter was in her crib, playing with her toys when it happened. She didn't want Sadie to see her grandpa like that, even if she was too young to understand what was happening.

"Well, you seem to be a good mom, Rose," Thorne said.

"Thanks for saying that," she said. She looked over at him and smiled.

"What?" he asked.

"Look at you—having a conversation and being nice and all," she teased.

"Shut the fuck up," he grumbled.

"Fuck," Sadie repeated from the backseat.

"Language," Rose shouted at Thorne. For the first time since she met the guy, he actually smiled, and she couldn't help but do the same. He had a nice smile, even through all the tough-ass exterior—not that she'd tell him that.

THORNE

THORNE HAD TO ADMIT THAT ROSE WAS GROWING ON HIM. Hell, he even thought that her kid was cute, and that might trip him up. His job was to keep Rose and the kid safe, not like them. He knew that getting too close to the person he was charged with protecting was a huge problem. It led to mistakes and miscalculations that could end up getting them all killed. He just had to remember that Rose wasn't someone for him to fuck around with. Savage wouldn't allow that, and he couldn't go against his club Prez that way.

When he was in the Army, he had been on a hell of a lot of ops that ended badly. He was one of the guys that the government would send in when they had exhausted all other possibilities. He was their last resort, and that usually meant going into a situation to find the people he was sent to save already dead. He was usually too late to save any of the victims, but that didn't matter to him. He knew that taking out his targets was what uncle Sam wanted him for, and he was damn good at killing. Hopefully, that wouldn't be a skill he needed to use in this case.

Finding out that a buddy was laying low in his safe house, Thorne had to come up with a plan B—fast. He called Savage and was told to take her to the place Bowie had out in Texas. Bowie's parents still lived out there, so they kept a house in Texas and let the guys in the club use it when they needed a place to lay low. It was off the beaten path and Thorne had to admit, he was thankful that Savage saved his ass. His club's Prez had a way of doing that—saving the guys in the club. He was the one who held them all together, but once in a while, he'd ask for help and not one of the guys would tell Savage no, even if it meant calling his boss and telling him that he'd need some time off. He'd do just about anything for Savage.

He brought in the last of their bags and piled them in the family room. "Which room should we take?" Rose asked, looking down at her daughter who was already finding her bags of toys.

"Um, I'm not really sure," Thorne said. "This place belongs to Savage. I guess you can pick whichever room you both would be comfortable in. Savage did mention that they have a kid's room here, so maybe Sadie would like to stay in there."

"I haven't slept without her since we left Joe," she admitted. "I've been too afraid that he'd catch up with us and take her."

"You don't have to worry about that here," Thorne promised. "Savage has a top-of-the-line security system. He's already sent me the specs on it. Also, no one will get in here without me knowing about it. You're both safe here," he said. He hated that Rose still looked skeptical even with his reassurances.

"All right," she breathed. "I'll try to let her sleep in her own room, but if she wants me, I'll bring her to bed with me."

"Whatever you want," he agreed. Honestly, he didn't care where the kid slept. He just wanted Rose to know that she was safe with him.

"Thanks," Rose said. "I'll get Sadie settled first and then, I'll check out the kitchen to see what we have to make for dinner."

"Bowie's mother ran over here and filled the fridge," he said. "If we need anything else, all we have to do is contact Savage and he'll have it delivered."

"He's being so kind to me, and that just makes me feel extra bad for not seeing him for so many years," Rose admitted.

"You don't have to feel bad," Thorne said. "I know Savage well enough to know that he wouldn't want you to feel bad about any of that. You're his family and to a guy like Savage, that means everything."

"Thank you for saying that," she said. "I guess I'll have to get used to having family again. It's going to take me some time though."

"You'll pick it up in no time, I'm sure," Thorne said.

She nodded, "Do you have any family?" she asked. He was afraid that making conversation with her might lead to her asking personal questions, but if they were going to be stuck together for an unknown amount of time, he was going to have to give her something.

"I don't have any family," he admitted. "My dad died about ten years ago, but we weren't close. My grandmother raised me, and she passed after I joined the Army." He left out the part about not knowing his mother. She had skipped out on him and his dad shortly after she had him.

"You were in the army?" she asked.

"I was, but I retired a few years back," he admitted.

"What do you do now?" she asked. This was the part that he usually tried to avoid answering. He'd give her the truth, but only a tiny bit of information to go with it—just enough to keep her from asking him more questions.

"I still work for the government—in the CIA. It's classified, mainly. What I can tell you is that my day job looks a lot like what I'm doing to help you," he said.

"So, you help people for a living?" she asked.

"I do," he said, even if it wasn't completely the truth. He usually was too late to save or help anyone, but he didn't want to tell Rose that. Thorne needed her to believe that he would do everything within his power to keep her and Sadie safe from her ex-husband. He needed her to trust him.

Sadie started to fuss, and Thorne was sure that he had never been so happy to hear a kid cry. "I better give her a bath and change her. She's probably tired and will want to go to bed early."

"How about you take care of her, and I'll make us all a

sandwich. That way we can all hit the hay early. I'm pretty beat myself."

"That would be great," Rose agreed. "Would you mind making Sadie a peanut butter and jelly sandwich?" she asked. "It's the only kind of sandwich she'll eat."

"Sure, no problem. It's my favorite too," he admitted.

"Great, I'll take one too, if you don't mind making three of them," she said. She picked up a small pink bag and her daughter, heading down the hallway. Thorne wasn't sure if he had told her too much about himself, but he had to admit, it was kind of nice to talk to someone besides the guys at the club.

He was kind of a loner. Besides taking the occasional woman home from Savage Hell for the night, he usually spent most of his nights alone, and that was just the way that he wanted things. He liked the fact that he didn't have anyone to answer to, but the nights sometimes got lonely, not that he'd ever admit that to anyone. Having Rose and her kid around wasn't going to be easy, but at least, it wouldn't be so lonely.

"I'm going to clean the peanut butter off of Sadie's face and get her to bed for the night," Rose said.

"When you are finished, would you mind meeting me in the family room?" Thorne asked. "We have a few things to talk about."

"Like what?" she asked, lifting the toddler into her arms.

"Like, what you can do to help me keep you and your kid safe," he said. She wasn't going to like most of the questions that he was going to have to ask her, but honestly, he had no choice. A part of him was curious about what had happened to her, but he also knew that the more information that he had, the easier his job to keep her safe would be.

"Fine, we can go over your rules, but I'm tired and will want to get to bed early," Rose insisted.

"Agreed," Thorne said. "While you put the kid down, I'm going to check in with Savage. I promised him that I would call back home with updates three times a day."

Rose nodded and disappeared down the hallway to the bedrooms. Thorne pulled his cell phone out of his pocket and dialed the bar. He knew that Savage would be at Savage Hell tonight with Bowie and that would be the best place to reach him.

"Hey, man," Savage answered. "Everything good?"

"Yeah, we got to the house a few hours ago and settled in. Rose is putting the kid down to sleep and I thought that I'd check in."

"I appreciate that, Thorne," he said. "How's Rose doing?" he asked.

"She's worried that her asshole ex is going to find us, even here. She wasn't happy that I destroyed her phone, but you were right, it was probably how he was tracking her. Honestly, I think that he won't stop looking for her, even without her cell phone. He doesn't sound like the type of guy who would just give up. Your cousin might be in deeper trouble than she's letting on."

"Shit," Savage grumbled.

"Yeah, she told me a little bit about her situation, but not all of it. I'm sure that there's more to the story than she's letting on, but I plan on talking to her about that tonight. Maybe she'll tell me the rest of it," Thorne said.

"Don't be surprised if she doesn't open up to you, Thorne," Savage warned. "She's a tough nut to crack, always has been, even when she was a kid. She's as stubborn as they come." Thorne had a feeling that was true, and probably why she had stayed with her ex for so long.

"I won't push her for more than she's willing to give," Thorne promised.

"I appreciate that, man," Savage breathed. "Keep me updated and let me know if we can help in any way. Just keep my cousin and her kid safe, man," he ordered.

"Will do," Thorne said. "You know that I will." Savage knew what Thorne did for a living and if he could help Rose and keep her and her kid safe, that's exactly what he'd do.

ROSE

"I think that I need more information about your ex," Thorne said.

"What?" she asked. They had been sitting across the room from each other, watching the nightly news ever since she had put Sadie down for the night. She should have just gone to her room and gone to sleep, but eight o'clock in the evening was way too early to go to bed for the night. Plus, she was too wound up from their long drive to go to sleep yet.

"Your ex, I need more information," he repeated. "If I'm going to be able to help you, I need more details."

"Like, what kind of details?" Rose asked.

"What did he do to you to make you leave?" Thorne asked. The last thing she wanted was to rehash what Joe had done to her. It was embarrassing that she didn't get out sooner, but she was an idiot for thinking that she'd be able to change him. She wanted things to work out with Joe because he was the father of her child. Rose was hoping that he'd change, if not for her sake, then for Sadie's

"I don't know why you're making me repeat this. I've already told you that we weren't married and that he abused me," she said.

"Right, but why did you finally leave him this last time? You said that he had beat you up before. So, what happened this time to make you leave?" he asked.

"I don't want to talk about this right now," she breathed. He was right—there was something that happened between her and Joe the last time he hit her, but saying the words out loud would make it all too real. She didn't want to admit that she was with a man who could say or do the things he did to her.

"I know that it might be uncomfortable for you to talk about your ex, but I have to know if I'm going to be able to properly protect you and your daughter," he reminded.

Rose took a deep breath and let it out if she was going to say it, she just needed to get it all out. "The last time he beat me, he told me that if I didn't get my ass back in line, he'd kill us both," she whispered the last part. How could a man kill his own child? "I couldn't take the chance that he meant it, so I grabbed Sadie and left."

"I don't blame you," Thorne said. "I would trust every word he told you—every threat. If he said he'd kill you both, he meant it. A man like that doesn't make a threat that he's not willing to keep."

"That's what I was afraid of, so I left him and never looked back," Rose admitted. Saying the words was easier than she expected it to be, but it still took a toll on her. Rose suddenly felt completely worn out and ready to sleep for days. "I'm really tired. Do you have any other questions for me?" she asked, knowing that she sounded a bit bitchier than she wanted to.

"Does he have any weapons?" Thorne asked.

"You mean, like guns and knives and stuff?" she asked.

"Yeah, that about covers it. Did he keep any in the home when you were with him?" he asked.

"Um, no," she said. "Well, nothing that I noticed. We had knives in the kitchen. I guess they could be considered a weapon." She thought about all the things she had to leave behind when she took Sadie and left.

"I really didn't go through his stuff," she said. "And when I left, all I cared about was packing stuff for Sadie and a few things for myself. I left everything else behind and ran."

"Where was your ex when you packed up and left?" Thorne asked. She tried not to think about that day too much, but she remembered it like it was yesterday and not weeks ago now.

"He left at nine to head to work on the morning that I left. I remember it because I had been up most of the night, nursing my black eye and busted lip. He had beat me pretty badly the night before and I finally reached my breaking point. That night, while I sat in the corner of our bedroom, watching him sleep, I thought about all the things that I could do to him to get him back for what he had done to me. I was sick of being his punching bag."

"That wasn't the first time he hit you?" Thorne asked.

"No," she almost whispered. "I thought that I could change him, and yes, I know how stupid that makes me sound. I stayed for my daughter's sake until I just couldn't stay anymore. He is a monster and there would be no changing that."

"No, there never is a way to change someone like that," Thorne said.

"You sound like you're speaking from experience, Thorne." He sat back and looked her over.

"I guess I am. We all have a little bit of a monster inside of us, don't we?" he asked.

"I don't believe that," she countered. "I don't know you very well, but you seem like a decent guy," she said.

"Yeah, don't confuse me being a good guy with me helping Savage out. I'm doing this because he asked me to, not because I'm a good guy." She felt a little hurt by his statement, but that was silly, right? She didn't know Thorne, so why should she be hurt that he didn't really want to help her out of the goodness of his heart? She went to her cousin for help, and Savage gave it. That was all that really mattered in any of this.

"Don't look at me that way, Rose," Thorne breathed.

"How am I looking at you?" she asked.

"Like I kicked your puppy," he said.

She smiled and nodded. "You read my mind," she teased. "How did you know that I was picturing you kicking my puppy?"

"Please tell me that you didn't bring a fucking puppy along with you," Thorne grumbled.

"No, but I was just trying to lighten the mood," she said.

"That's not what this conversation is about," Thorne said. "I need to know what I'm going up against. You told me a little bit in the car, but I need more details."

"Well, he didn't have any weapons that I noticed when we lived together. What's your next question?" she asked, trying to sound more business-like.

"Do you have a formal custody agreement with the guy— you know, something saying that he can see Sadie?" Thorne asked.

"No, as I said in the car, we were never married. His name is on the birth certificate, but he never sued me for physical custody of her, but I wouldn't put it past him. That's why I went to Savage for help. I wasn't sure what to do. I mean, I can't run forever but there is no way that I'm going to give that asshole my daughter, even if a court tells me to. I can't do that to her. Sadie is innocent in all of this. She can't help it that her father's an abusive twat. It was my choice to be with him and it's my decision to get her as far away from Joe as possible."

"Abusive twat," Thorne repeated, "and, here I thought that you didn't cuss."

"I never said that I don't cuss. I just said that I'd prefer that you not do it in front of my daughter. I try to be the best version of myself for my daughter and if that means holding my tongue and not cursing, then so be it."

"I'll try to do better, but I can't make any promises," Thorne said.

"You pointed that out in the car, on the way here. I appreciate any effort that you're willing to make, Thorne," she said. "Do you have any other questions for me?"

He nodded, "Besides your cell phone, is there any other way that your ex might be able to track you?"

"Unless he's sewn trackers into our clothing, I don't think so," she said. "I ditched my car at Savage's place, and he said that he'd hide it, just in case anyone came looking for it. Sooner or later, Joe might put together that Savage and I are related. I didn't tell him much about my family, but as I've already said, he has money and resources to find me. He'll turn over all the stones that lead to me, and I'd hate for Savage and his family to get hurt in the process."

"You never have to worry about him getting to Savage. He's got a lot of guys at Savage Hell who have his back. They'd all give their lives for him. Plus, Savage is pretty bad ass and can take care of himself. Don't worry about him. He's been through a bunch of shit and come out on the other side."

"Yeah, that's one of the reasons why my father warned me to stay away from him. He and Savage's father had a falling out when I was just a teenager. My father told me to stay away from him, and honestly, left me no choice but to obey him."

"What kind of falling out?" Thorne asked.

"I'm not sure. I don't remember much of the fight. My

father accused his father of stealing the love of his life away, and I've always wondered if he was talking about Savage's mother. I mean, I don't remember my uncle being with any other women. If my suspicions are true, then I feel bad for my mother. She died when I was a kid and I know that she loved my father like mad. She used to tell me that he was the best man she had ever known. If Savage's dad stole the love of my father's life, then he wasn't talking about my mother, and I guess that just makes me sad for her."

"Yeah, that would suck for your mom. I'm sorry that your father and Uncle's fight tore your family apart, but it's great that you and Savage have each other now." It was pretty great that she had the guts to find Savage and ask him for help, but they had a long way to go before they'd be a part of each other's lives again. Heck, she didn't even catch all his kids' names when he introduced them to her earlier.

"I hope that once this nightmare is over, we'll be able to get to know each other again. So much has changed since we last hung out," she said.

"I bet," Thorne said. "Listen, I'm going to lock up and check on everything before heading to bed. You good?" he asked. Thorne stood from the sofa and damn it—she couldn't stop herself from looking him over. He might be older than the men she usually dated, but he was hot as sin and made her think about doing things with an older man that she shouldn't think about.

"Nope, I'm good," she lied. Her nerves were on edge and now, she was thinking dirty thoughts about a man who was almost old enough to be her father. Yeah, she was definitely not all right.

"Night, Rose," Thorne said on his way into the kitchen. He didn't bother to look back at her and she had no reason to be butt hurt about that fact, but she was.

THORNE

SAVAGE HELL MC

THEY HAD BEEN TRAPPED AT THE SAFE HOUSE FOR WELL OVER two weeks now and Thorne hated how much he had come to like Rose. He went to bed every night thinking about her and woke up every morning excited to see her. They had been eating every meal together and he thought that it might be nice to ask her to have dinner with him after Sadie went down to sleep. He really wanted to call their dinner a date, but he also knew that doing so might scare Rose off and that was the last thing he wanted—especially with how close they were becoming.

"There you are," he said, finding her playing with Sadie in her room.

"Yeah, I put Sadie down for a nap, but she had other ideas. She found me in here folding laundry and demanded to help." He smiled at the toddler who was sitting in the

36

empty clothes basket, the floor littered around her with clean, unfolded clothing.

"I can see that she's being a big help," he said.

Rose giggled and the sound rang through the room. "Yeah, she's usually a huge help when it comes to housework, but I appreciate that she tries."

"Well, I wouldn't mind giving you a hand," Thorne offered. Rose had been washing most of his clothes with hers and Sadie's. It was strange having someone take care of something like that for him. Rose said that she felt she owed him for all the help he had given to her and Sadie, but he hated she felt that way. She owed him nothing, but he appreciated her helping him out.

"You don't have to do that," Rose said, as he grabbed a handful of clothes from the floor and started folding them. He wasn't sure how she liked things, but he could at least give it a try. She watched him as he folded Sadie's little pajamas and laid them on the bed with the other folded clothing. When Rose didn't make a move to correct what he had done, he felt a crazy sense of accomplishment.

He knew that this was his chance to ask Rose to have dinner with him as they quietly folded clothes together. "Um, I was thinking," he started.

"Oh, I don't know you well enough yet to think that's a good or bad thing," she teased.

"It could go either way," he joked. "But I was thinking that we should have dinner together tonight."

"Okay, but I don't know why you're thinking about that. We have dinner every night together," she countered.

"Well, yeah, but I was thinking that we could have a nice dinner—you know just the two of us once Sadie goes to bed." Rose looked at him hurt and he instantly regretted his words.

"You don't like eating dinner with Sadie?" she spat.

"That's not what I'm saying. I was just saying that it might be nice to have dinner just the two of us," he said again. He wasn't sure if he was screwing everything up, but from the look on her face, he knew that was the case.

"I'm not sure that's a good idea," she whispered. "I'm not ready to date anyone yet. Plus, I don't know when Sadie will go down and I wouldn't want to hold up your dinner." That was a lie—Sadie went to bed every night at the same time for the past two weeks. He was pretty sure that the kid would be asleep by eight, just as she was every night. She hated that she was using Sadie's bedtime as an excuse not to have dinner with him. She was turning him down, and that felt like a kick in the gut, not that he'd tell her that. They stood in silence as they finished folding laundry. He looked over his shoulder to find that Sadie had fallen asleep in the laundry basket, and he couldn't help but smile at the toddler. She was a pretty cute kid.

"Oh," Rose breathed. "I better put her in her bed. Um, thanks for helping me fold the laundry." She was dismissing him, and he could take the hint.

"Anytime," he grumbled, walking out of her room. Rose might have shot him down, but he wasn't done trying with her. Thorne had a feeling that Rose might be worth the trouble.

Rose had put Sadie down almost an hour ago and had been avoiding the kitchen since. Thorne had spent most of the evening perfectly grilling the ribs that he had marinated all day in the refrigerator. Thorne had thrown a couple of baked potatoes on the grill with the ribs, and he also made a giant salad, figuring that he needed some greens, and that Rose might appreciate the effort of his making a salad.

He sat down at the table with the giant plate of ribs just as she walked into the kitchen. "I was going to ask you if you changed your mind and would like to have dinner with me, but you've made it very clear that you're not interested in anything like that," Thorne said. Yeah, he was being an ass, but he just couldn't help himself. Asking Rose to have dinner with him tonight, just the two of them, and having her turn him down hurt like a bitch. He loaded his plate up and started eating while Rose stood there and watched him.

"It's fine," she almost whispered. "I'll have a peanut butter and jelly sandwich, check in on Sadie, and then go to bed. I'm exhausted," she said. Shit, now he felt bad for acting like an ass. What was it about this woman that made him feel like he needed to apologize every other minute?

She turned to go out of the kitchen, and he sighed, pushing the plate of ribs back from himself. "Rose, wait," he ordered, surprised that she obeyed him. "I'm sorry. I'm being an ass."

"Yes," she breathed, "you are, but it's fine. I wasn't very nice when I told you earlier that I wasn't interested in dating you. I know that I probably hurt you and that wasn't my intent. I just assumed that you were asking me out, and well, I guess I have my defenses up when it comes to men. I'm sorry that I mistakenly jumped to that conclusion." She hadn't mistakenly jumped to any conclusion. Honestly, he was asking her to have dinner tonight with him as sort of a date. They had spent the past two weeks, getting to know each other, and well, it had been a damn long time since he had dinner with a pretty woman. He could blame it on temporary insanity from the smell of her strawberry shampoo. But he liked her, and it didn't really have much to do with the scent of her shampoo.

"How about you skip the peanut butter and jelly sandwich and eat some of these ribs? I won't be able to finish them all myself and I made a salad and everything. I know how much you love salad."

She giggled and nodded, "I do love salad," she agreed. He could tell that she was thinking his offer over.

"If it makes you feel better, we can just consider this a late-night dinner—nothing else," Thorne assured.

"I am hungry," she said as if talking herself into his offer.

"Great," he said, standing from his chair. He pulled out the chair next to his and she slid into it.

"Thank you," she breathed. He handed her a plate and waited for her to load it up before digging into his food.

She nodded to his beer, "Do you have another one of those?" she asked.

"Um, yeah," he said. Thorne stood and walked over to the

fridge, pulling out a couple more beers, and handing her one. "I didn't have you pegged as a beer drinker," he said.

"Well, I don't drink a whole lot when I have Sadie. I mean, I'm all she has and if I'm incapacitated and she needs me, that's not fair to her, right?"

"No, it's not," he agreed. "You're a good mom, Rose," he said.

"I don't need you to say that, Thorne. I'm just a single mom, trying to get by while doing the best that I can."

"I think that you're more than getting by," Thorne said. "I don't say things that I don't mean. You're a good mom."

"I appreciate that, Thorne," she said. "Some days, I feel like I'm doing a really good job, you know? I mean, she seems happy and all. But then, there are days when she's fussy and I'm crabby about it, and well, I just feel like a failure."

"I think that's what makes you a good mother, Rose. I mean, if you got it right every single day, you'd probably be doing something wrong. Everyone has days when they feel like they're failures, but you get up and keep on trying. That's all you can do, right?"

"I guess, I've never thought about it like that," Rose admitted. "Joe liked to point out my faults. He liked to tell me how I was failing not only him but our daughter. I guess that I started to buy into what he was saying."

"We've already established that your ex is an ass, so I think that you should stop believing anything that he's told you in the past," Thorne said.

"That's easier said than done," Rose insisted. "I mean, if I was able to just block out all the hateful things he's ever said to me, I probably wouldn't have stayed with him for so long." Thorne knew enough victims to know that was true. They usually believed the person abusing them and ended up staying for much longer than they ever should. Some of the victims never made it out of the relationship alive. Those were the ones who had stuck with him. Those women were the ones he wished that he could go back and save somehow, but he couldn't. Thorne was too late to save any of them, but he could help Rose, and that's what he needed to focus on right now.

"I believe you," he said. He stood from the table and cleared both of their plates. "It couldn't have been easy to live that life. You were smart to get out when you did though."

"Thanks for saying that," she said. Rose stood and brought the half-empty platter of ribs to the kitchen counter. "Um, I don't mind doing dishes, since you cooked," she offered.

He handed her a towel. "How about you dry, and I'll wash?" he asked. The whole scene was so domestic that after a few minutes of them working together in unison, he found himself wanting to spill his guts to her. "I've never done dishes with a woman before," he admitted.

She giggled, "Not even your mother?" she asked.

"Um, no," he said. "I never really knew my mother. My grandmother raised me since my father wasn't around a whole lot. She used to like to push me out of the kitchen before I could get 'Under her feet,' as she liked to say."

"I'm sorry that you never got to know your mother," Rose said. "I guess that's something that we have in common. I was so young when my mother died, I didn't really know her either."

"My mom split shortly after I was born. My father blamed himself, but I never understood why. She said that she didn't know what she was getting into when she agreed to marry him and have a kid. She said that she wasn't ready for what having a baby entailed and she just left."

"That sucks," Rose breathed. She dropped her towel to the kitchen counter and put the last plate away in the cabinet. "Raising a baby is hard. I had my dad to help me for the first year and a half of Sadie's life. If it wasn't for him, I don't know how I would have made it through her infant stage."

"I don't believe that for a second," Thorne said. "You're such a good mother."

"Thank you for saying that, but it's true. I had no idea what I was getting myself into when I had her. Of course, I didn't agree to it or anything like that. Sadie was a happy accident and one I'll never regret, no matter who her father is."

Thorne dried his hands on the towel that she had thrown on the counter and turned to face her. "I like you, Rose," he almost whispered. Thorne cleared his throat wondering what the hell was wrong with him. He was acting like a middle school-aged boy and all he wanted to do was tell the pretty girl that he liked her.

"Um, I like you too, Thorne. You're a good guy, and you're really sweet to offer to help Sadie and me," she said.

Rose was pushing him off, and that wasn't what he wanted. Every time she thought he was making a move on her; she'd shut down or deflect. Usually, he let her do just that, but this time, he wanted to push her for more just as much as she wanted to push him away.

"Rose don't do that," he said.

"Do what?" Rose questioned.

"Don't push me away. I like you and I know that scares the hell out of you, but I had to tell you. I'm not asking you to be my girl or spend your life with me. I just wanted you to know—I like you." Rose nodded and he thought that was going to be the end of their conversation, but he should have known better. Rose was going to make excuses and come up with reasons why he couldn't like her, but it wouldn't change a thing.

"I've already told you that I'm not ready for something to happen with you or any man right now, Thorne," she started. He wasn't about to stand there and list the reasons why he couldn't like her. He did the only thing he could think of doing, under the circumstances. He pulled Rose against his body and sealed his mouth over hers. He expected a fight, but she didn't give him one. Instead, Rose seemed to melt against him and when she wrapped her arms around his neck, he knew that he had finally pulled down a small section of the wall that she had put up.

He broke the kiss, leaving them both breathless and she looked up at him with a mixture of desire and being completely pissed off at him. "Why did you do that, Thorne?" she asked.

"I told you—I like you," he simply repeated as if that would explain his crazy behavior. He didn't make it a habit of going around and kissing women who obviously didn't like him back. But with Rose, he just couldn't help himself.

"I told you that I like you too, but I'm not ready for something like what you just did, Thorne," she said. "Listen, if this is going to be a problem, I can call Savage and ask him to send someone else or let me come stay with him." The thought of Savage sending someone else to watch over Rose and Sadie had him seeing red. The last thing he wanted playing through his mind was Rose kissing another man in the safehouse while he took care of her.

"You can't go stay with Savage and his family," Thorne said, trying to talk some sense into her. "You'll only bring danger to their doorstep, and he wouldn't ever allow that to happen. I agreed to watch over you and take care of you and Sadie, and that's what I'll continue to do. This won't be a problem, Rose. I won't let it be a problem. In fact, you have my word that I won't touch you again, not even if you begged me to." He sounded like an ass, but he just didn't care. Having her turn him away hurt like a bitch and he wasn't going to stand there and pretend that it didn't.

"Well, you don't have to be such an ass about it, Thorn," she spat. Her anger was something that he could take. It was the hurt look in her eyes, every time he made his move, that he hated. "And you don't have to worry about me begging you to touch me because it's never going to happen," she spat.

"Good to know, princess," he breathed as he brushed past

45

her. He was going to steer clear of Rose as much as possible and hope like hell that Savage got something on her ex soon because their living arrangements just became unbearable.

ROSE

ROSE KNEW THAT DENYING HER FEELINGS FOR THORNE WAS only going to end up with her getting herself in deeper than she wanted. She liked him, but she was also afraid of making another mistake. So, she gave him a song and dance about not being ready to date, and that was probably true, but the fact of the matter was—she really liked Thorne. He seemed like a nice guy, but sometimes, they were the ones you needed to watch out for.

Over the next few weeks, Rose found herself trying to avoid Thorne as much as possible. She thought that might be the best course of action, but she was wrong. Every day that passed seemed to end with Thorne being grumpier and grumpier. He'd offer to have dinner with her every night and when she refused, telling him that she had made something for her and Sadie earlier, he'd mumble something about giving up, or why bothering to try. She pretended not to hear him, but she had. Thorne was frustrated by her behavior, and why shouldn't he be? She was treating him badly when all she wanted to do was tell him that she'd love to accept his dinner offer and then end up in his arms at the end of the evening because it was getting harder and harder to resist her feelings for him.

She walked into the kitchen after putting Sadie down for the night and found Thorne sitting at the table, eating his dinner alone. He had made chicken on the grill, and it smelled so good, that her mouth watered. "Hi," she breathed.

"Hey," he mumbled around a mouthful of chicken. "I'd ask if you want some chicken, but I wouldn't want you to think I'm asking you out or anything."

Rose smiled and sat down at the table across from him. "Actually, I'd like some chicken," she admitted. He looked her over as though he didn't believe a word she was saying, and she grabbed the plate of chicken and pulled it toward her.

"You weren't kidding," he breathed.

"Nope—I love barbecue chicken. This smells so good. Do you mind?" she asked, nodding to the plate to make sure that she was still welcome.

Thorne stood and she was sure that he was going to leave the room, much as she had done to him over the past few weeks every time he asked her to join him. That would serve her right, but instead, he crossed the room to the cabinets, pulled out another plate, and handed it to her. "Help yourself," he said.

"Thank you," she said, taking the plate from him and helping herself to some chicken.

"I have left over salad from last night if you want some. I only wanted meat tonight. I'm kind of sick of vegetables," he admitted.

"I'd love some salad," she said. "Thanks for this."

"No problem," Thorne said. He got the salad out of the refrigerator and handed it to her. "It's pasta salad."

"You know, you're a really good cook," she said.

He chuckled, "You haven't even tasted my food yet," he reminded.

"Well, from what I see here, you are an excellent cook." He sat down across from her, and she took a bite of the chicken, followed by one of the pasta salad. "I was right," she said with a mouthful of food. "You are a good cook."

"Thank you," he said.

"You know," she breathed, "I don't really know much about you. I mean, you seem to know a good deal about me, since you had to know about my ex and our relationship, but you really don't talk about yourself."

"Yeah, well, there isn't much to tell," he said.

"Oh, I don't believe that for a second," she said. "You seem like an interesting guy. How long have you known my cousin?" she asked.

"I've known Savage for about ten years now. That's when I moved to Huntsville and found the Royal Bastards. Walking into Savage Hell was the best decision that I ever made. I patched in and from that moment on, Savage and the guys have become my brothers. I don't know what I would do without any of them."

"I can understand why you feel that way," she said.

"Savage is a great guy. I'm just sorry that we grew apart because of our fathers."

"Yeah, Savage is the best," he breathed.

"What brought you to Huntsville?" she asked.

"Work," he said. "When I moved there, I was still active in the military. I had to report to Redstone Arsenal and when I went into the CIA, I just stuck around."

"What exactly do you do?" she asked.

"It's complicated and sometimes, it's classified. Let's just say, I'm the guy they send in when no one else wants the job," he said.

"What kind of jobs are we talking about?" she asked.

"Murder, kidnapping, that kind of thing. I'm who they send in to get people out. A lot of the time, I'm too late, but then, I have to go after the bad guys and take care of things."

"Take care of things?" she croaked. Rose was starting to wonder just who her cousin had sent to protect her and Sadie. She knew that he was capable, but not deadly.

"I make sure that they are good and dead so that they can't hurt anyone else," he said.

"Oh," she breathed, "I had no idea."

"Yeah, well, it's not something that I like to share. Most of the guys at Savage Hell don't even know about what I do for a living. Not that it would matter. Most of them are either active-duty military or retired. We all have our specialties, mine just happens to be killing people."

"Well, hopefully, you won't have to kill anyone while you're with me," she said.

"Rose," Thorne breathed, "you do know that I'm nothing

like him, right?"

"Like whom?" she asked, although she already knew the answer. She did know that he was nothing like Joe. Thorne was kind and patient—two qualities that her ex never possessed.

"Your ex—I'm nothing like him," Thorne said.

"I know that, Thorne," Rose whispered, "and, I'm sorry that I treated you like you were. I guess I just needed a little time to come around to the fact that I like you. I was afraid of making another wrong decision and the last one nearly destroyed my and Sadie's lives."

"Wait—you like me?" Thorne asked. He dropped his fork to his plate and pushed it back from himself.

"I didn't want to admit it, but I do like you, Thorne," she said.

"Is it so awful to admit?" he asked. He sounded like he was hurt by her declaration, but she wanted to tell him the truth.

"Not awful," she said. "Scary. It's scary to put myself out there again, you know?"

"I'd really like for you to give me a chance, Rose, but I won't push you for one," he admitted.

"I'd like to give you a chance too, Thorne," she whispered. "I'm just not sure how to do it."

He smiled at her, "Well, I think that I can help with that," he said. "Do you think that you can trust me?" he asked. That was the question of the evening. She wasn't sure if she could trust herself, but she was sure that trusting Thorne was something that she already did.

"I trust you already, Thorne," she admitted.

"Good," he breathed, "then, come here, Rose." She liked the fact that he didn't ask her if she wanted to go to him, he just told her what to do. Thorne patted his lap, and she knew that he wanted her to sit. She didn't hesitate, standing from her seat to sit on his lap. Thorne banded his arms around her and nuzzled his face into her neck. God, he smelled good—like a freshly showered man.

"You smell good," she whispered.

"Thanks, you do too," he said. "You always smell like strawberries. I'd really like to kiss you, honey. Are you good with that?"

"I am," she whispered. "I want you to kiss me, Thorne. In fact, I'd love for you to kiss me." He didn't waste another second, sealing his mouth over hers. She couldn't help her moan in his mouth as she wrapped her arms around his neck.

He broke their kiss, leaving her breathless. "What now?" she asked, hoping that he'd be willing to continue to call the shots.

"Now," he whispered against her lips, "I'd like to take you back to my bed and make you mine. Are you good with that?" he asked. Rose nodded her head and he growled. "Give me the words, honey."

"I'm good with that, Thorne. I want you to make me yours." Rose wasn't quite sure what that would entail, but she was up for whatever Thorne had planned for her. She wanted to be his and so much more.

THORNE

THORNE WASN'T SURE WHY HIS LUCK HAD CHANGED, BUT ROSE finally giving him a chance was like a fucking dream come true. She kissed him like she couldn't get enough of him and all he wanted to do was take even more from her.

He stood from the kitchen chair, never letting her out of his arms, carrying her back to his bedroom. Thorne had fantasized about having her in his bed since they got to the safehouse. Every night that she went into her room across the hallway from his, he longed to tell her how much he wanted her in his bed.

He sat on the edge of the mattress with her still in his arms, and when Rose turned and straddled his lap, wrapping her arms around his neck, he wanted to push her under his body and take her. Pushing her too fast might be something that he'd regret, but he needed her.

He rolled her under his body and kissed her. "Tell me

now if you want me to stop," he begged. He didn't want her to ask him to stop, but he needed her with him.

"I don't want you to stop," she said. "I want you, Thorne."

That was all the green light that he needed. Thorne worked his way down her body, stripping her as he went. "You taste good," he breathed as he kissed his way down her torso. "I need to taste you everywhere though," he whispered against her tummy.

"Thorne," she whimpered. "Please." She seemed to be completely on board with whatever he wanted from her, and he planned on making her feel good.

Thorne settled between her legs and pulled her panties down her thighs, spreading them as he went. He was going to make a meal out of her, and she seemed to want that as much as he did. He licked his way through her wet folds, and she nearly bucked him off the bed.

"Hold still, honey," he breathed against her pussy.

"I can't," she whimpered. He pressed her into the mattress, holding her in place as he continued to eat her pussy. He had her shouting out his name in no time and when she begged him to stop, he gave her one more orgasm.

"I need you," she shouted as he made her come on his tongue. She was perfect and hearing her say that she needed him made him want to give her exactly what he was asking her for.

He kissed his way back up her body and Rose pouted at him. "You're still wearing clothes," she said. Thorne stood from the bed and tugged his shirt over his head.

"Better?" he asked. She looked him over and smiled. He

knew what most women saw when they looked at him—a hard-ass biker with a ton of tats and even more scars. But when Rose looked at him the way that she was, it was as though she saw him differently. She seemed to be able to look past all of that and see inside his soul. She seemed to see the real him and if that didn't scare her off, Thorne didn't know what would.

"Much better," she agreed. "Now, the pants." He unzipped his jeans and pulled them down his thighs. "No underwear?" she asked.

"Nope," he breathed. "I don't like them."

"Yeah, I can see why," she said, eying his cock.

He put his hands over his manhood and took a step back from her. "Jesus honey," he grumbled. "You keep looking at me like that and this will be over before we even get started."

"Oh, we've already gotten started," she teased. "I'm already past getting started. Come here, Thorne," she said, giving him back his words from earlier. Everything about Rose was sexy but hearing her tell him what to do was a complete turn-on. He did as she ordered and walked back over to the bed. She sat up and wrapped her small hands around his cock, causing him to hiss out his breath. Having Rose touch him was everything he never knew that he needed or wanted.

"Does that feel good?" she asked.

"Yes," he hissed. "It feels perfect, but if I let you keep that up, I'm going to come in your hands, and I want in your pussy."

"I'm on the pill," she whispered.

"I can still use a condom if you want me to," he offered. The last thing he wanted was for Rose to feel like he didn't protect her. It was his job to keep her safe, both in and out of the bedroom.

"That's up to you, but I'm covered and I'm clean," she breathed. He didn't need any more of an invitation. Thorne pushed her back against the bed and covered her with his body, pressing her into the mattress. He gave no warning when he filled her and when she wrapped her legs around his ass, he nearly lost his load. He wasn't going to last long, not with Rose doing everything in her power to make him crazy.

"This is going to be fast," he whispered.

"That's okay, we have all night," she countered.

"God, you really are the most perfect fucking woman on the planet, aren't you?" he asked.

"Far from it," she said, "but for you, I want to try to be." She wrapped her arms around his neck as he pumped in and out of her body. It didn't take him long to build to his release and when he came, he shouted out her name, collapsing onto the bed next to her.

"Thank you for trusting me," he whispered, pulling her against his body. Thorne pulled the blanket up over the both of them as she snuggled her ass against his cock. "Tease," he said.

She giggled, "Can I sleep in here with you tonight?" she asked. There was no way that he planned on letting her out of his bed.

"Yep," he said. "In fact, I'd like for you to move in here with me, honey."

"What about Sadie?" she asked.

"She has her own room," he said.

"No, I mean, I don't want to confuse her." He didn't want to upset the toddler either.

"How about we work around her schedule? You can be here with me when she doesn't need you. Sooner or later, she'll get used to us being together, honey," he assured.

"Okay," she agreed. "I'll move in here with you as long as you're good with me laying down with Sadie when she has a nightmare or something. Sometimes, she needs me in with her."

"Absolutely," he agreed. "You're calling the shots here, Rose. You tell me what you want when you want it, and I'll make it happen."

She turned to face him. "Really?" she asked. "Because I think that I'd like to try that all again," she said.

He pulled her against his body and kissed her. "You really are the perfect woman, honey," he breathed against her lips.

ROSE

Rose pulled her cell phone from the nightstand, trying to silence the offensive ringtone that she uploaded for when Savage called. She hoped that she'd be able to climb out of bed without waking Thorne, but when she looked over to find his handsome face staring back at her with a grumpy expression, she couldn't help but laugh.

"Sorry," she whispered.

"Who the fuck is calling you at four in the morning?" he asked.

"Um, it was Savage. I silenced it and can go into the other room to call him back. You should go back to sleep," she insisted.

He got out of bed and pulled on a pair of sweatpants. "Not a chance," he growled. "If Savage is calling you at four in the morning, he has his reasons. I need to know what they are." He pulled her back down to the bed, to sit next to him, and she shook her head at him.

"You really don't need to be on every call that I make to my cousin, you know?" she asked.

"Just fucking call him back, Rose," he ordered. Normally, she'd give him some fight when he ordered her about like that, but she was too tired and honestly, a bit worried about Savage's early morning phone call. Thorne was right—it couldn't be good news that Savage was calling to give her at four in the morning.

"Fine," she grumbled, calling him back.

"Rose," Savage said on the other end of the call. "I'm sorry to call you so early." She could hear it in his voice that something was wrong.

"What's happened?" she asked.

"I got a call from your ex's lawyer," Savage said. "He's asking to see you."

"Asking to see me, for what?" she asked. "Why would his lawyer reach out to you? How did he even know to contact you?" A million more questions ran through her head, but she shut up to let Savage answer some of them.

"Well, we have the same last name, so I'm thinking that might be how your ex's lawyer found me." She sometimes forgot that Savage was her cousin's last name too, and not his first name. It wouldn't take much to hunt Savage down if they knew her father's name. Joe knew her father's name and he'd stop at nothing to find her and Sadie.

"Hey, Savage," Thorne said. "I'm here with Rose. Why do you think he got his lawyer involved?"

"I'm guessing that he wanted to keep things on the up and up. If he's trying to get custody of Sadie, he can't just show up at our place and demand to see Rose. He's going through the proper channels, and I bet that has everything to do with wanting to look good in case he has to make a court appearance." Shit, that was the last thing she needed—for Joe to come off as a "Good guy" in court. She'd lose her daughter and that would destroy her.

"He can't take my daughter," Rose breathed. "It will kill me."

"We're not going to let him take Sadie, Rose. You have my word," Thorne said. He pulled her into his arms, and she wanted to feel the comfort he was giving her, but she couldn't. They didn't know Joe like she did. He wouldn't give up coming for her and Sadie. He wouldn't rest until he destroyed her for leaving him.

"Thorn's right," Savage agreed. "We won't let him touch you or Sadie ever again."

"I appreciate that, guys," she said. "But I don't know how you'll be able to stop him. Maybe if I meet with him, we can come to some understanding." She knew that it would be a losing battle she'd be fighting, but that might be the only way.

"No fucking way," Thorne shouted. "There's no fucking way that I'm going to let you meet with that asshole."

"You don't get to forbid me to see someone, Thorne. I have my own mind and can make it up for myself," Rose spat.

Thorne cleared his throat, "I think we'll need to call you back, man," he said. Rose knew that he was going to give her a fight and didn't want her cousin listening in while he did it. That was just fine with her. It didn't matter who was listening in, she wasn't going to let any man tell her what to do—not ever again. Being with Thorne had given her the courage to stand up for herself—even if it was her ex that she'd be taking a stand against.

"Okay, call me back once you two make up your minds about what you want to do," Savage ordered. "Although, I have a feeling that I already know what you're going to decide." He ended the call and Rose wondered what he meant by that.

Thorne took her phone from her hand and tossed it onto the bed. "We need to talk," he insisted.

"About?" she asked, already knowing exactly what they needed to talk about.

"Don't be cute, Rose," Thorne grumbled.

"Well, I'm not sure how else to be," she teased.

"You can't be serious about going to meet with your ex," he insisted.

"But I am serious about going to see him. I really need to fix this mess that I'm in so that we can go home. I won't let Joe rule what I can and can't do in my life anymore. Being with you has given me the courage that I need to face him," she said. "I think that it's time for me to press charges against him and stand my ground. I have photos on my phone, and I think that it's time for me to share them." She had never shown anyone those photos—she couldn't because every time she looked at them, they made her feel sick. She was ashamed of every black eye that she allowed Joe to give her, and it was time to take a stand. Waiting around for Savage to find something on her ex wasn't working for them. She was sure that he was involved in some illegal shit, but she just couldn't wait for Savage to uncover it any longer.

"Are you sure that you want to do that, honey? You have nothing to prove to me or anyone else," Thorne said.

"I know that, but I need to prove to myself that I'm strong enough to stand up to Joe. I can't keep running. You have a life to get back to and so do Sadie and I," she said. Thorne hadn't made her any promises, and she didn't ask him for any. She knew that what they had going on was probably just sex to him but the thought of going back to her life wasn't something that she was looking forward to. Life in the safe-house with Sadie and Thorne had become something that she could see herself wanting even after she was safe from Joe. But she couldn't ask Thorne for more—could she?

"What does that mean?" Thorne spat.

"It means that you've already given up more than you probably thought you would have to. When Savage asked you to help me out, you probably thought that it was going to be for a few days, maybe a week or so—not months. I'm sure that you have things to get back to," she said. "What about your job?"

"Nope," Thorne said. "I had a ton of time off with the CIA. Plus, I only take jobs that I want to take. I don't have to ever work again if I don't want to because I've been well compensated for my so-called skills," he said. She knew what Thorne did for a living. He went in to help people that no one else could help. He was skilled at killing—that's what he had told her when she first asked him about what he did for a living.

"Well, I'm sure that you miss your friends and want to get back to Huntsville," she insisted.

"I'm not sure what you're doing here, honey, but I'm just fine where I am. What's up with you, Rose?" he asked.

She sighed, rethinking even bringing it up. "I guess I'm just worried that when this is over, you'll go back to your life, and I'll go back to mine." She felt like an idiot for saying what she was thinking out loud. She sounded like one too.

"I guess I haven't given you much to go one about what we're doing here, honey," he breathed. Thorne pulled her against his body, and she thought that her heart might beat out of her chest.

"What are you doing?" she asked. Every time he touched her it was the same. He made her ache with need. She'd never tell Thorne this, but she'd do whatever he wanted when he touched her the way that he was.

"I'm setting things straight. I should have done this from the start, Rose," he said.

"You don't have to—" He covered his hand over her mouth, and she couldn't help but look up at him.

"I need to get this out," he said. She nodded and he dropped his hand from her lips. "I don't really fool around with women. In fact, if I do take a woman home from the bar, it's for one night and one night only."

"I don't need to hear about you and other women," she mumbled.

"I'm not going to tell you about me and other women,

because there are no other women," he insisted. "I'm not with you because you're a convenience for me or because there's no one else around. I want you, Rose, all of you. Hell, I even like your kid," he said.

She giggled, "Her name is Sadie," she reminded.

"I'm aware," he said. "The little monster has grown on me, just like her mother has. I don't want to go back to my life because I don't want that life back. I want you, and if that means that we have to figure out what life outside of this house is going to look like, I'd like to figure it out with you."

"You would?" she asked.

"I would. I didn't make this clear, but when you got into bed with me, you became mine. I plan on keeping you, Rose," he whispered into her ear.

"You do?" she asked.

"I do," he repeated. "Are you good with that?" he asked.

"I am," she said without hesitation. "But none of this changes the fact that I'll need to meet with Joe. He won't stop coming for Sadie and me if I don't give in and do what he wants."

"I don't want you to ever have to see that fucker again, honey," Thorne growled. She felt the same way, but how else was this mess going to end unless she did what Joe wanted?

"I don't see any other way," she said. "What if you come with me?" she asked.

"That's just going to piss your ex off," Thorne warned, "but, I'm in. I won't let you talk to him alone, and you seem hell-bent on settling things with him."

"I am," she said. "It's the only way to end this. Plus, once

Joe realizes that I'm not afraid of him anymore and that I have evidence that can put him away for a while, maybe he'll leave Sadie and me alone." She knew that she was hoping for something that probably wouldn't happen, but she needed a little bit of hope right now. Without hope, she was doomed to live a life in hiding, and even though Thorne just made her a very pretty promise, he wouldn't wait around for her forever. That was just too much for her to hope for.

THORNE

Savage had set up the meeting between Rose and her ex for the next day and he had to admit he wasn't looking forward to any of it. He had tried to talk Rose out of going to the meeting, but she refused to listen to him. Savage had sent reinforcements to the meeting. He and Bowie showed up along with a few other guys. They had picked a place halfway between Huntsville and Austin, where the safehouse was. If things went south, Savage said that he didn't want Joe to know where he could find them. That worked for Thorne because keeping Rose safe was his focus.

Bowie agreed to stay back at the hotel with Sadie and keep her safe, promising that if they needed to get out of there fast, he'd meet Thorne and Rose back at the safe house with her. Rose didn't seem to want to leave her daughter behind, but she knew that it would be safer for her with Bowie. There would be no way that Thorne would give Joe what he wanted—and that was Sadie. He knew that not bringing the guy's daughter along, as he had requested, was only going to piss him off, but Thorne didn't really give a fuck.

They drove to the meet-up at an abandoned parking garage, and Thorne could tell that it was a set up before he even got out of his truck. "Stay in the truck," he ordered.

"Why, what's happening?" Rose asked.

"I think that your ex is playing games and I don't want you getting out of the fucking truck. Can you just listen to me this one time, Rose?" Thorne asked.

"You don't have to be an ass about it," she spat. "Why do you think we're being set up?" she asked.

His cell phone chimed with an incoming message, and he pulled it from his pocket. He read the text from Savage and handed her the phone. Rose gasped as she read the message out loud. "He got Sadie," she breathed. Savage's message said that Joe had shown up to the hotel room, knocked Bowie out, and took Sadie. That was his plan all along.

"He lured us out of the room just so he could get to Sadie. He knew that I wouldn't bring her along and he planned this whole time to take her," Rose sobbed. "We fell for it too. I told you that I should have stayed behind with her."

"And what would you have done when Joe showed up to take Sadie?" Thorne asked. The thought of her facing her ex alone scared the hell out of him. She was right though. He had let her down. Allowing Joe to get to Sadie was on him, and now, he needed to get Rose's daughter back or he was sure that she'd never forgive him. Hell, he wouldn't be able to forgive himself, but that was something that he didn't want to consider. Right now, he had to call Savage and get a plan together. They were going to have to get an Amber Alert put up before Joe was able to leave the state with Sadie. Otherwise, he might not ever find her.

"I know that you need someone to blame right now and that I'm it, but I'm already blaming myself enough for the both of us. You need to remember that I do this kind of thing for a living. If someone needs saving, I'm the one people hire to do the job. I'll find Sadie, Rose, and then, I'm going to fucking kill your ex."

"You can't do that," Rose insisted. "You'll go to jail." He sent her a look and she sat back. "I forgot that you're good at killing," she almost whispered. He regretted telling her that, but she was right—he was good at killing. If he wanted to kill her ex and have no one ever find out about it, he could do just that. The question was—if he killed Joe would Rose and Sadie be able to forgive him?

He got in touch with Savage, and they agreed to meet back over at the hotel. Bowie had called the police and when they pulled into the hotel parking lot, Thorne cursed at the amount of cop cars and ambulances sitting there. "They're going to let the whole fucking world know what went down here," he grumbled.

"Isn't that what we want?" she asked. "To let the world

know that my asshole ex took my daughter. Isn't that how we're going to get her back?"

"This many cops on the case will only hold things up. I'll need to find whoever is in charge and cut through the rest of the red tape." Thorne knew that time was of the essence if they were going to get an Amber Alert out. "They'll want to talk to you. Do you think that you can handle that?" he asked.

"I'll be fine," she said. "I just want my baby back."

"We'll get her back," Thorne promised. "While you're answering questions, I'm going to find the right guy to help me get an Amber Alert up. It will help us to find her quickly."

"Okay," she said. "I'm sorry that I lashed out at you earlier. I was the one who demanded that I meet with Joe. I should have seen this coming, but I was so focused on getting us back home, that I never imagined that he'd double-cross me and take Sadie. I guess I'm just mad at myself. I shouldn't have shouted at you."

"Honey, you can shout at me all you want to. I'm the one who should have seen this coming. I failed you, but I promise that I'll find Sadie and bring her home to you. Do you trust me?" he asked. Thorne felt as though he was holding his breath waiting for her to give her answer.

Rose nodded, "I do trust you, Thorne," she assured.

"Thanks for that, honey," he breathed. "Ready?" he asked.

"As I can be," she said. He helped Rose out of his truck and disappeared into the hotel room to find Savage after one of the officers started questioning her. He felt awful leaving her alone to face their questions, but he needed Savage's help to find whoever was in charge of the investigation.

"Hey," he said, walking into the hotel room. Bowie was sitting on the edge of the bed with Savage next to him, and an EMT was looking over the bloody lump on Bowie's forehead. "You okay, man?" Thorne asked.

"I will be," Bowie assured. "I just need a few stitches and then, I'm going to find the asshole who did this to me. I'm so sorry that he got Sadie," he said.

"This isn't your fault," Savage insisted. "We should have seen this coming. I mean, the guy wanted his daughter. It was the perfect way for him to get to her and hurt Rose in the process. We just need to make sure that we get Sadie back from the asshole. Then, we'll fucking kill him," Savage added.

"Yeah, that was my idea too, but Rose is against us killing the fucker. I think she believes that justice will be served, but I'm just not sure. First, we have to find him though. Do either of you guys know who's in charge here?" he asked.

Savage pointed out the door to some guy smoking a cigarette, standing by a police cruiser. "He seems to be the one that they all answer to," Savage said.

"Good, I'll be back in a few," Thorne said. He walked out of the hotel room to find the guy stomping out his cigarette butt on the pavement. "I hear that you're the one in charge here," Thorne said.

"Depends on who's asking and what you want," the guy said.

"The name is Victor Thorne," he said, pulling out his wallet to show the guy his CIA credentials.

"I see," the guy breathed, "what can I do for you Mr. Thorne?" he asked.

"You can help me get an Amber Alert up for Sadie Savage," he insisted.

"You want to do that?" the guy asked. "She was taken by her father."

"Right—her father who's an abusive asshole who has threatened to kill his own daughter and her mother." He nodded over to where Rose stood, still answering questions.

"I saw the two of you show up here together. Are you with Ms. Savage?" the detective asked.

"I am, and she has evidence to prove that her ex abused her. She's been living on the run since leaving her ex and she's ready to press charges against him." He watched as the detective seemed to think over his options. "You and I both know that once he leaves the state, he's going to be damn near impossible to track. He attacked a friend of mine to get to his kid. I think that you'd want to find and keep him here in your prison system, since it happened in your state, under your watch." Yeah, he was hoping that pissing the detective off and playing to his ego might actually help get him moving in the right direction. It was a dangerous game to play, but he really had no other options. The police around there seemed to have one speed—slow motion, and that wasn't going to help him out at all.

"Fuck off," the detective grumbled. "I'll put out a damn Amber Alert, but I'm telling you to steer clear of this investigation." That wasn't going to happen, but Thorne would agree to just about anything to get the detective moving.

"I'll sit this one out," Thorne lied. "Besides, I won't put Ms. Savage in danger, and going after her ex would do just that. Thanks for your help, detective," Thorne said. He turned to head back into the hotel room as the guy pulled his radio from his belt buckle. He called in the Amber Alert and Thorne smiled to himself. They were going to catch the fucker who took Sadie. This gave them a fighting chance and once he could convince Savage to put one of his guys on Rose, to sit on her while he went after Joe, he'd be on his way. There was no fucking way that he'd be sitting this one out—not when his future with Rose was on the line. And it was.

ROSE

Rose paced the new hotel room that Thorne had lured her into. She had no idea that he planned on dumping her off with a babysitter and going after Joe and Sadie himself. She should have seen the signs. When they got to the hotel, he said that he had forgotten something in his truck and when he was gone for way too long, she opened the door to find one of Savage's buddies guarding the door to the hotel room.

Of course, she demanded that he let her out of the fucking room so that she could go find her daughter, and he handed her a phone, pushing the button to call Savage. She took the phone and pretended that she was surprised to hear her cousin on the other end of the call, but she wasn't. He, Thorne, and Bowie had gone after Joe, chasing down leads from the Amber Alert that had been placed for her daughter. Thorne had called in some favors and was being fed all the information by one of his informants.

Stomping her foot and shouting at them to circle back to get her, wasn't her finest moment, but she just didn't care. She told Savage that it wasn't fair that she wasn't involved in looking for her daughter and even threatened to never talk to him again, but she didn't mean it. Her cousin seemed to know that too because he stood his ground, refusing to let her in on the search for her daughter. And there was no way that she was going to sit around and wait for news about Sadie.

Rose walked over to the room's only door and opened it, finding Savage's guy still standing guard. "Um, I need to get some fresh air," she said. "I'm feeling a bit claustrophobic in here."

"Savage said that you need to stay put," the guys said. She could tell that she was going to have to lay on the charm if she was going to win this guy over.

"I'm sorry, but I didn't catch your name," she said, smiling up at the biker.

"That's because I didn't give it," the guy said. "I'm not here to talk to you. I'm here to keep you safe," he insisted.

"Well, I really appreciate that," she said. "Whatever your name is."

"It's Yonkers, but you knowing my name isn't going to change the fact that you don't get to leave your room, princess," he said.

"Not even for a second," she pouted. "I just need to stretch my legs and breathe some fresh air. It's so stale in here." Yonkers looked a bit torn about what to do, and even though she should feel bad about what she was doing, she didn't.

"Please," she begged, laying it on a bit thick, even for her own liking.

"Fine, but I'm going with you," he insisted.

"Thank you," she squealed. "I'll do whatever you say. Just let me grab my jacket. She had one shot at this, and she wasn't going to blow it. Would you mind if we stopped in the lobby so that I could grab a snack? I'm starving."

"Sure, I guess I should have offered you something to eat, sorry," he said.

"Not a problem," she lied. "I know you were just doing what my cousin told you to do." She grabbed her purse and flung it over her shoulder, feeling the weight of the handgun that she had packed in there before Thorne, and she left Texas with Sadie in tow. She knew that pulling her gun on poor Yonkers wasn't going to be fair, but she honestly had no other choice. If she was correct, the pickup truck parked down by the lobby was his. If she could just get close to it, she'd get his keys, even if she had to threaten him with bodily harm. Rose wasn't a violent person, but this guy didn't know that. When it came to her baby, she'd do whatever it took to find Sadie—even holding up the big biker and taking his truck keys from him.

"You got everything you need?" he asked.

"Yep," she breathed, patting her handbag. "I'm ready." She followed him to the end of the corridor and down the steps to the first floor. The place only had three floors and they were on the second. "Do you mind if we grab some air first?" she asked. "Then, we can walk around to the lobby to grab a snack on the way back up to the room."

"Sure, whatever you want," Yonkers said. "Just stay behind me." That wasn't going to be a problem for her. She'd stay behind him the whole time since it would give her time to get her gun out of her handbag. She fumbled with the zipper and by the time she finally got her bag open, they were in front of the truck. It was now or never.

"Stop," she almost shouted. "Turn around," she ordered. Yonkers quickly spun around and gasped when he saw the gun in her hand.

"Where did you get that?" he asked. "You shouldn't have that, you'll hurt yourself."

She barked out her laugh, "Why?" she asked, "because women can't use a gun? I was taught how to use one of these when I was just a kid. Hurting myself shouldn't be what you are worried about, Yonkers. I think that you should be more focused on me hurting you."

"You wouldn't," he said.

"Oh, I would. You all think that you can keep me from going after my daughter, but I'm not the sit-back-and-wait kind of girl that my cousin and Thorne have mistaken me for. I want to know where they are."

"I can't tell you that," Yonkers insisted.

"Okay, if you won't share that bit of information with me, how about you toss me your truck keys? I'll go find them myself," she spat.

"You can't do that," Yonkers said. "If you do, you'll just be in the way. Plus, you'll never catch up to them."

"How about you let me worry about that?" she asked.

"Or," a man's voice said from behind her, "you can hand

me the gun and I'll let you see our daughter." Shit—she had fallen for yet another one of Joe's traps. She was an idiot to believe that he'd leave her behind and just take Sadie. When he promised to kill her, he said that he'd end them both.

She turned, pointing her gun at Joe. He held his gun steady and pointed at her chest, and she knew that they were in a standoff that wouldn't end well for either of them. "Joe," she breathed. "Where is Sadie?"

He nodded back to his truck where her daughter was watching the whole scene. She was crying and the thought of Joe laying one finger on Sadie made her want to pull the trigger. "She's all right, for now. How about you be a good girl and come with me so that we can have a little chat, Rose?" Joe asked. If she went with him, they might both end up dead, but it was a chance that she was willing to take to get to her daughter. Rose had to do everything in her power to keep Sadie safe. She owed her daughter that much.

"Fine," she spat, "I'll come with you."

"You can't do that," Yonkers shouted.

"Who the fuck is this, Rose?" Joe asked. "Is this piece of shit your new boyfriend?"

"What—no," Rose said.

"You can't go with him, Rose," Yonkers repeated.

"She can do whatever she wants," Joe said. "Are you going to stop her?"

Yonkers stood to her side and nodded, "If I have to," he said.

"Well, good luck with that," Joe grumbled. He shot Yonkers; the bullet hitting him just above his chest, below his shoulder. If she was right, he had gotten lucky and the bullet went straight through, not hitting anything major. Yonkers cursed as he fell backward, landing on the pavement.

"Let's go Rose, or I'll finish him," Joe shouted, holding out his free hand to her. She didn't take it, but walked toward her ex, knowing that he was good at keeping his promises. He said that he'd find her and Sadie if she left him, and he had.

"I'm so sorry, Yonkers," she sobbed as she turned back to look at him.

"We'll find you, Rose," Yonkers promised. The mean look on his face showed his determination, and she knew that he'd make good on his promise too. The guys finding her was the only hope that she had that she and Sadie would get out of this mess alive.

They drove well past nightfall and Sadie fell asleep in her car seat. Rose was thankful that her daughter seemed to calm down after she got into the truck with her and Joe. She looked fine, but until she got a chance to carefully check her out, Rose worried that Joe had done something awful to their daughter.

"Did you hurt her?" she whispered, trying not to wake Sadie.

"No," he breathed, "you think so little of me, don't you, Rose? You never even gave me a chance. You destroyed us before we even had a chance to be a real family. That was all I ever wanted."

"We both know that isn't true," she insisted. "You were the one who destroyed our family," she said. "You were the abusive ass who beat me up every time I so much as stepped a toe out of line. You were the one who destroyed us, Joe, not me." She knew that standing up for herself would only end up pissing him off, but she honestly couldn't sit there and listen to any more of his lies. He only saw things the way that he wanted to—never the truth.

"I'm going to let that lie go, Rose," he said. "You've been under a lot of stress lately and I think that your cousin and his gang of misfit bikers has brainwashed you into believing the worst of me. You just need to remember how things really were between us."

"Oh, there is nothing wrong with my memory, Joe. I remember everything that you did to me and what you threatened to do to Sadie if I ever tried to leave you. No one has brainwashed me, and I don't need to be reminded of anything about my past with you. That's exactly where our relationship belongs—in the past," she said.

"Have it your way," Joe said. "I just thought that you'd like the chance to be a family with Sadie and me, but I guess I was wrong. Our daughter and I will be just fine without you." The thought of Joe raising Sadie without her scared the hell out of Rose. She couldn't back track now. Joe would see straight through her. The only thing she could do now was hope that Savage and Thorne would find her. Joe made one critical error when he doubled back to town to take her—he gave the guys his exact location and more time to catch up to them.

"How exactly did you find me?" she asked. "We changed hotels and everything."

His smile was mean, "I never really left once I took Sadie. I followed you and your new biker friends, and when I saw you walking around the outside of the hotel, I felt like my luck was finally changing. I didn't want to leave Sadie in the truck alone to come in and get you."

"You're such a good father," she sarcastically drawled.

"I know that you don't mean it, but I'm going to take it as a compliment anyway. I am a good father, and any judge would see that," he insisted.

"Sure, and after Yonkers testifies that you shot him while kidnapping me, the judge will surly award you custody of our daughter," she drawled.

"Jesus fucking Christ, Rose," he shouted, startling Sadie from her sleep. The toddler started to cry, and Joe's frustrated growl filled the truck. "Why do you always have to question me and put me down?" She hated it when he got this way. Joe was a grown man throwing a fit like a child. She already had to deal with one toddler, she didn't need another. Why did he think that his tantrums would make her see things his way? They had the opposite effect on her, not that she was about to tell him that now. It would only serve to make him angrier.

She soothed Sadie, promising her that everything was going to be all right, even though that might not be a promise she'd be able to keep. "So, what's the plan here, Joe?" she asked. "You thinking about getting rid of me and keeping our daughter?" she asked. She really didn't want to give him any ideas, but she also wanted to keep him distracted and talking, to give the guys some time to find them.

Rose had pulled her cell phone from her pocket and dialed Savage. It was the only saved number in the phone and although she couldn't tell if her call had gone through, she had nothing else to hope for—she just prayed that it did.

"I'm thinking about it. I mean, with all these woods around here, I'm betting no one would find your body for some time," Joe proudly said. He was boasting about disposing of her body and all she could do was hope that Savage and Thorne were listening in too.

"Where are we going? Where are you taking us?" she asked.

"That's nothing you need to worry about," Joe said. "Just sit back and enjoy your last ride. We'll get there soon enough." She looked back to find Sadie sound asleep again and was actually relieved that if he did decide to kill her and dump her in the woods, her daughter wouldn't have to witness it.

"Why did you have to go and leave?" he almost whispered his question.

"I left because I didn't want to have to deal with your abuse anymore. You threatened to hurt Sadie, and I couldn't let that happen. You left me no choice but to leave you, Joe," she said.

"I'd never hurt Sadie," he assured. "She's a part of me. Unfortunately, she has a part of you in her too, but she'll forget all about you once you're out of her life. Don't worry,

I'll never tell her about you, Rose. I wouldn't want to ever disappoint my daughter."

"She's my daughter," Rose spat. "You've never even changed a diaper."

"A nanny could change her diapers. I don't need you to do that anymore," Joe insisted.

"Sadie has been potty trained for two months now," she said. "As her father, you should know that."

"Whatever, just sit back and shut the fuck up, Rose," Joe said. She could tell that arguing with her seemed to take a toll on him, but she wasn't going to rest until Joe was out of her life for good. Maybe Thorne had the right idea—Joe needed to die.

As if on cue, Sadie woke up crying that she needed to use the potty and she knew that this might just give her the chance to escape. If Joe stopped at a rest stop, she'd be the one to take Sadie to the potty since Joe wanted nothing to do with that kind of thing.

"You can hold it," Joe told her.

"She can't," Rose challenged. "She's only been going potty for two months. If you make her hold it for long, she'll pee in the car seat and then, you'll have a real mess on your hands."

"Fine," he spat, "there is a rest stop about a mile up the road. Can she hold it that long?" he asked.

"She should be good," Rose assured. "We'll find a potty in a few minutes, honey," Rose promised. "Just hold it for Mommy." Sadie whimpered and nodded her little head. Rose spotted a mile marker and knew that this might be her only chance to give the guys her exact location. "There," she pointed at the rest stop sign, "it's right up there off of mile marker twelve."

"I can see that for myself," Joe grumbled.

"I was just trying to be helpful," Rose insisted. She was trying to be helpful, but not to him. She wanted to help Thorne and Savage find her, and hopefully, they'd be able to do just that now with this new information. Her life depended on it.

THORNE

"SHE'S SUCH A SMART GIRL," SAVAGE PRAISED, "ALWAYS HAS been. Rose just told us exactly where she is." Thorne put the mile marker in the GPS and when he saw that they were only two miles behind her, he told Savage to go faster. "We'll get to her," Savage promised.

"I know, but she can't stall him forever. This might be our only chance to get both Rose and Sadie back from that asshole," Thorne said. Once he got them back, he planned on never letting them go again.

"She won't have to. All we need is for Rose to take Sadie to the bathroom and stay there with her. She's smart enough to know to do that. Then, you and I can take care of Joe." Thorne knew exactly how he wanted to take care of Joe, but he also made Rose a promise that he wouldn't kill her ex.

"I'm going to call this into the detective who put out the Amber Alert for Sadie," Thorne said.

"You think that's a good idea?" Savage asked. "How will we explain him taking Rose too?"

"I'm not explaining anything to him," Thorne said. "They should have put one of their guys on Rose and not just assumed that Joe was done with her." Honestly, he was kicking himself for not doing that same thing. He hated that he had only left Yonkers with Rose. He should have stayed behind too, but he wanted to be the one to bring Sadie back to her. It was his promise to her, and he wanted to keep it. He just never thought that Joe would be bright enough to double back and take Rose.

He pulled out the detective's business card and called the number on the bottom. As soon as he answered, Thorne didn't give him much time to talk. "This is Victor Thorne. We've found Sadie and Rose. They are at the rest stop off of mile marker twelve."

"Did you say Sadie and Rose?" the guy asked.

"I did," Thorne admitted, "her ex doubled back and took Rose too, and shot one of our guys in the process. She somehow snuck a call to her cousin, and we've been able to listen in on their conversation. Her ex plans to kill her and dump her body in the woods. Her daughter had to go to the bathroom, and he agreed to pull over. We don't have much time. We're about a half a mile away now."

"He's armed," the detective said.

"Yeah, he shot one of our guys who was guarding her back at another hotel. We moved her, but I'm guessing that asshole was watching us the whole time," Savage shouted.

"Don't engage," the detective insisted. "I'll have my guys

there in five minutes." There was no way that Thorne or
Savage was going to sit in the damn truck and wait for Joe to
load Rose and Sadie into his truck and take off again.

"Fuck that," Savage growled. "When we get to the rest
stop, we're getting Rose and Sadie out of there. If that fucker
tries to stop us, well, you can just clean up the mess once you
get there. We're not waiting."

The detective protested and Thorne ended the call, not
wanting to listen to the guy bark orders at them. Savage was
right—Saving Rose and Sadie was the most important thing.
The rest was just static.

They pulled around to the back of the small building,
finding Joe standing guard in front of the ladies' room door.
He wasn't going to let anyone in or out without his knowl-
edge. "We'll have to see if there is a window around back,"
Savage said. He cut the lights and engine, parking behind the
building. They walked to the back of the ladies' room to find
one small window. Thorne knew that he and Savage wouldn't
be able to fit through it, but Sadie and Rose could probably fit.

Savage gently tapped at the window and there was no
movement on the other side. "What if they've gone back out
the front?" Thorne asked.

"Or they've found a way to escape without you two meat-
heads getting involved," Rose said, standing behind them.
She was holding Sadie on her hip and Thorne was sure he
had never seen a more beautiful sight.

"You got out," Savage said. "I told you she was smart."

"Yeah, you can play proud cousin later," Rose said. "Right

now, I need you two to get us out of here before Joe finds out that we're not in that bathroom. I'd say that we have about two more minutes." Shit—that didn't leave them very much time.

Thorne grabbed Sadie from her and started for his truck. "Savage, you drive," he ordered.

"No problem," Savage agreed.

"What happens if he sees us?" Rose asked.

"I think that they'll take care of Joe for us," Thorne said, nodding to the half dozen police cars that entered the parking lot.

"You guys called the cops," she breathed.

"Yeah, you wouldn't let me kill your ex, so I did the next best thing. With Yonker's testimony that Joe shot him, and your testimony about him kidnapping you and Sadie, and all your evidence of him abusing you, he'll go away for a long time."

"I'm finally going to be free?" she asked.

"You will be if they catch him. He's taking off for the woods," Savage said. "You stay here with Rose and the kid. I'm going to stop him."

"Savage," Rose shouted after him, but her cousin didn't stop or turn around. He took off for the tree line, putting himself between Joe and the cops. "He's got a gun," she whispered.

"He knows, honey," Thorne said. "Savage can handle himself." Thorne just hoped that he was right, because the big guy was a hot head, just like his cousin. Savage liked to dive into the deep end headfirst and worry about the consequences later.

Thorne watched as Savage practically lunged at the guy, knocking him to the ground as he went. Within seconds, cops were surrounding them both, cuffing Joe and holding Savage until the detective walked across the field and nodded at them to let him go.

"They got him," Rose sobbed.

"Yep, they got him, honey," Thorne said. "You can go back to your life now. You don't have to go into hiding again."

Rose turned and snuggled into his body. "You mean, we can go back to our lives now. Remember, you promised that I'm yours and that you want a life with me and Sadie. Is that still true, Thorne?" she asked. It was always going to hold true for him. He'd never stop wanting a life with Rose and Sadie.

"It's still true," he admitted.

"Good," Rose said, wrapping her arms around him. "Then, how about you take us home with you, Thorne? I think it's about time that we start our lives together and I'd like to do it back in Huntsville."

"I think that your cousin would kill us both if you wanted to live anywhere else. He's already found a house for you and Sadie." Thorne said. He had found them both a great house in town—perfect for Sadie. It even had a swing set in the backyard.

"Well, then, it will be the perfect house for the three of us. How about it, Thorne? You want a fresh start with me?" she asked.

"I'd love nothing more, honey," he agreed. He pulled her up his body to kiss her and Savage cleared his throat.

"I'm afraid that I'm going to have to break this up," Savage said. The detective was by his side and nodded to Rose. "You'll have a lot of questions to answer."

"I'm ready to answer them all if it means that Joe will be out of our lives for good," Rose agreed.

"You don't have to worry about that, Ms. Savage," the detective said. "He's going away for a long time." That was the best news Thorne had heard in a damn long time.

"Would you mind following me to the station, Ms. Savage?" he asked.

"We all will," Savage agreed.

"I'd also like to have Sadie checked out," Rose said. "Joe said that he didn't do anything to her, but I don't believe a word he says."

"Of course," the detective agreed. "I'll have an ambulance meet us at the station."

"Thank you," Rose said. "Do you think that we'll be able to go home in the morning?" she asked the detective.

"I think that can be arranged," the detective agreed.

They were waiting outside the ambulance for Sadie while Rose gave her statement. Rose made him and Savage promise not to leave Sadie's side, and he didn't plan on it. The toddler was pretty happy, all things considered. Savage was making faces at her, causing her to squeal with laughter and Thorne wondered if he'd ever be that good with the kid.

"She really likes you," Thorne said.

"She's a Savage," he said, "she knows I'm one of her people and that's why she laughs at me. My kids are the same way," he said.

"I wonder if she'll ever like me as much," Thorne admitted. Saying out loud made him sound like a pussy.

"She will," Savage assured, "you just need to give her a chance to know you."

"Yeah," Thorne agreed.

"Speaking of," Savage said, "you and my cousin seem to have gotten cozy."

"We have," Thorne said. If Savage was about to give him shit about his being with Rose, Thorne didn't care who he was. He'd still set his club's Prez straight.

"What are your intentions?" Savage asked, sounding like her father more than just her cousin. "I'm all the family she has left, so I think it's a fair question."

"It is," Thorne agreed. "I plan on marrying her, but I don't think she's ready for that next step. She's agreed to us moving in together, so that's huge. She's been through so much, I think that I just need to take me time with her, but I'm in love with her, man," he admitted.

"Good to hear," Savage said. "And yeah, I think that taking your time with her is a good idea too. But she'll come around. Like I said, my cousin is smart."

"Why am I so smart now?" Rose asked, joining them.

"She looks good," the EMT said as Rose climbed onto the

ambulance to be with her daughter. "I don't see any signs of abuse."

"Thank you so much for checking her out," Rose said. She scooped Sadie up into her arms and Thorne helped her climb back down from the ambulance.

"How did it go in there?" he asked.

"Oh, it was fine," Rose said. "I had to answer a ton of questions, but Joe is being held without bail since he's a flight risk."

"That's great news," Savage said. "How about I take Sadie over to the truck and get her buckled in. she looks tired. I've gotten us a couple of hotel rooms nearby and then, we can all head back to Huntsville in the morning, if you're up for a road trip."

"I'm more than ready to go home," Rose agreed, "but, what about all of our stuff at the safehouse?"

"Bowie's mom has already been out there and packed everything up for you guys. She shipped it back home to my place. I'll run it by your new house once it is delivered."

Rose went up on her tiptoes and kissed Savage's cheek. "Thank you for everything," she said. "We'll be right over." Savage walked across the parking lot to Thorne's truck and started to put Sadie in her seat.

"So, we're going home," Rose said.

"Looks that way," Thorne agreed.

"I have a small confession to make," she said.

"Oh?" he asked.

"Yeah, I overheard you and Savage talking about the two of us moving in together," she admitted.

"I see," he breathed. Then she had heard the part about him wanting to marry her too.

"You love me?" she asked.

"I do," he said, "and, I want to marry you, honey, but only when you're ready."

"Well, what if I told you that I think that I might be ready now?" she asked. He wasn't sure if he should get his hopes up or not, but he was.

"You mean it?" he asked.

"I do," Rose said. "I might still have a lot of demons to fight, but I was hoping that you'd want to help me fight them together. How about it, Thorne, you want to make me your wife?" she asked. He wanted that more than he wanted anything in his life.

"I'd love to call you my wife, honey," Thorne said. He pulled her into his arms and sealed his mouth over hers. He wasn't sure how it happened, but he had fallen for the sexy little hell cat and now, she was going to be his forever— Thorne's Rose.

The End

What's coming next from K.L. Ramsey? You won't want to miss Spider (A Halloween Novella- Royal Bastards MC: Huntsville Chapter Book 12)!

SPIDER

Spider sat in the beat-up old truck that he used when he was working undercover. He hated that heap of shit. God, what he wouldn't give to have his bike, but he couldn't give too much of his real-life away—not with the group of assholes that he was working with. They were the worst of the worst and there was no way that Spider would let any of his true identity out for them to see. He saved riding his bike for days when he knew that he was going to be alone or at least able to fly under the radar. But since the new chain of command was in town, taking over where Chains left off, that wasn't going to happen for a while now.

What he really wanted was a home-cooked meal and a hot shower—and God, he'd kill to be in his own bed for a night. Instead, he was stuck sleeping in his crappy old truck, waiting for orders from the new leader of the Ghosts. Hangman wasn't the most pleasant guy to be around, and

Spider usually avoided him at all costs. But when the Ghost's new leader asked for him specifically, he had no choice but to say yes.

When he took this assignment, going undercover for the CIA to bring the Ghosts down from the inside, he knew that he was getting into bed with the devil. He just never knew that removing one devil led to a few others popping up in their stead. Since he had been working undercover, the Ghosts had lost four leaders. Hangman was just the next one up for the job, and Spider wondered what his new so-called boss would have him doing before the end of the night.

Spider caught the shadow outside his truck door, and before he could react, Hangman was standing outside his window, holding a gun to his head. "How about you tell me why you're just sitting here?" Hangman asked. "You were supposed to meet me at the warehouse."

"That's not what I was told, boss," Spider drawled. He was sure that he hadn't gotten their meeting place mixed up, but he was dog tired and there was always the possibility of a screw-up. He prided himself on always having his head in the game and never fucking directions up. It was what had kept him alive this long, living in two very different worlds. He never felt fully present in his real life anymore. Hell, he had spent so much time undercover with the Ghosts, that he forgot that his other life even existed at all.

"I don't give a fuck what you thought you were told," Hangman spat. "Slide over, I'm driving," he ordered, opening the driver's side door to Spider's ancient truck. He didn't argue, sliding over the bench seat to the passenger side of the truck and buckling his seatbelt into place.

"Where are we going?" Spider asked.

"Back to the fucking warehouse, where you were supposed to be in the first place. We have a new shipment of women being delivered tonight and it's time for you to earn your paycheck." Shit—the last thing that his CIA operative told him was that the deal the Ghosts had made, to bring in more women to sell at auction, had been killed.

"You're getting another shipment?" Spider asked, trying to keep up.

"Yeah, and I need you there to help with them. I know how much you love to babysit our new captives," Hangman said. Spider fucking hated taking care of the new women that they'd kidnap and brought in for auction. They were all terrified and he had to play the part of the asshole who mistreated them. He hated every fucking second of it if he was being honest. The whole process made him sick, but it was also what kept him going, trying to bring down the Ghosts without getting caught.

"Yep," Spider agreed, "I just hope that some of them are lookers this time. The last batch wasn't really my taste."

"I don't pay you to fucking taste the merchandise," Hangman growled. That was a good thing and the only way that Spider stayed under the radar. If they were expected to handle or "Taste" the merchandise, as Hangman said, he would be found out for being a mole because there was no way that he'd be able to bring himself to do that to one of those poor women.

"Got it," Spider agreed. "No tasting the merchandise. So, how long will they be at the warehouse?" he asked. As long as Hangman had the cells full at the warehouse, Spider would be expected to stay and guard them. If he got lucky this time, they'd be there for more than a few days and he'd be able to get a message to his operative at the CIA. He'd love to finally bust the Ghosts for human trafficking and be able to move on to a new case. It had been over two years that he had been with the Ghosts, and he was beginning to get restless.

"A couple of days and then, I'm thinking of having you move them for me," Hangman said.

"You want me to move them?" Spider asked. He had never been given such a responsibility before. Hangman usually used his upper guys to move the goods—men who had been with him before he was even a Ghost. He trusted those men and honestly, he had no reason to trust Spider. He shouldn't trust him because if given the chance, Spider would have his asshole boss behind bars in seconds flat.

"Yeah, Butch is unavailable, and I need you to take the lead on this one," Hangman said. Shit—Butch was his right-hand guy and if he was off doing another job while the CIA did their raid of the warehouse, they'd never catch all the top players. He'd be the one in charge of the merchandise which meant taking out Hangman would be for nothing. Sooner or later, Butch would take his place, and the cycle would continue. Spider wanted to ask Hangman why him, but that would do him no good. Questioning the boss was never a good idea and would probably end up with him dead in a ditch somewhere. That's what happened the last time he questioned his boss. He ended up having to stage his own death, letting his MC brothers think that he was dead for over a year, to be fully initiated into the Ghosts. He had to prove himself and becoming a literal ghost was the requirement.

"You good with that, Spider?" Hangman asked.

"Yeah, I'm good with it," he lied.

"Great, now let's haul ass over to the warehouse. I want to get there before the truck arrives. You'll need to count and assess the girls while I pay the guy." God, he hated this fucking job, but sooner or later, he'd get his break and bring down Hangman and the entire Ghost organization. He'd just have to be patient, which was not his strong suit.

"Sure, boss," Spider agreed.

AMELIA

Amelia Goodwell wasn't sure how she had ended up in the back of a truckful of other women, being taken in the middle of the night, but here she was. The last thing she remembered was dancing the night away with her best friend, Sandy, at their favorite little nightclub in town. Her town was so quiet usually that the one nightspot on Main Street really drew a crowd on Friday nights. She and Sandy were supposed to stick together, but she never imagined that she should have her friend follow her to the ladies' room. But going alone was her biggest mistake ever and one that she wasn't sure that she'd live to regret.

She looked around the truck at the other women's faces, noting that she remembered some of them from the club, but didn't really remember any of their names. The one thing she was sure of was that Sandy wasn't in the back of the truck and that meant that her best friend would be involving the authorities to help track her down. It was the thought that she held onto that gave her hope as she spent countless hours bouncing around the back of the truckful of women.

"Where are they taking us?" the scared-looking woman sitting next to her asked. She had been crying for most of the ride—something that Amelia felt like doing herself, but she was practical when it came to things like that. She knew that crying would do her absolutely no good.

"I don't know," she admitted.

A woman sat up in the corner of the truck and moaned, grabbing her head. "I think someone put something in my drink," she slurred. That much was very clear to Amelia. She felt like her skull was going to split open and every time she tried to focus, her stomach roiled in discomfort, and she felt about ready to puke. She had never personally been roofied before, but she was pretty sure that this was the way that it felt.

"Why would someone do this to us?" the woman next to her cried. She had no answer for her again, but she wished that she did. Amelia looked around the truck again and realized that all the women in there with her were of a certain age—young, and attractive. It crossed her mind that whoever took them was going to do something unspeakable with all of them, but how could that be? She had heard of things like this happening to other women but never imagined that it would happen to her. Things like this didn't happen to women like her.

Amelia was a lowly personal assistant at a local law firm. Her life was quite boring compared to other women she knew. Hell, she spent most of her free nights at home, in her pajamas, watching some lame television show until she was tired enough to go to bed. She was the most boring twenty-two-year-old that she knew. The only time she really broke out of her shell was when she and Sandy would go to the club to let off some steam.

The truck stopped and the woman next to her whimpered. Amelia reached for her hand and held it in her own, trying to silently let her know that everything was going to be okay, even if she had a sick feeling that it wasn't. The back doors of the truck swung open to reveal three big men, all mean-looking and pointing guns at the women.

"Let's go, ladies," one of the men shouted at them.

"Where are we?" someone from the back of the truck asked.

"You keep your fucking mouths shut, and no one will get hurt," another man warned. Amelia didn't quite believe him that their silence would guarantee their safety, but she also knew when to keep her mouth shut. It was a skill that she learned at an early age.

Her father wasn't the easiest man to get along with. He drank too much and when he did, he was mean. He liked to slap her mother around, and when she finally took off, leaving Amelia and her younger sister with their alcoholic father, he decided that they'd do in a pinch. She became a punching bag for her old man and took most of the punishment so that her sister could be spared. That was when she learned that silence was golden, even if it didn't always stop her father from hitting her.

"Now, I'm going to say this one more time, ladies," the first man spat. "Let's go." She stood, knowing that he wasn't going to give her or any of the other women another chance to comply.

Another truck pulled up next to the men holding guns at the women, and two more men jumped out. The one driving looked to be the one in charge. He started barking orders as soon as he got out of the old truck. The second guy looked the women in the truck over and seemed a little bit green by the whole scene. If she wasn't mistaken, she noted a hint of pity in his dark eyes and that surprised the hell out of her. None of the other men looked at the women that way. They seemed to look straight through them, not really even seeing them. Maybe it was easier for the men that way. They wouldn't have to think of the women as human beings, but as objects that needed to be moved at any cost.

"Where are you taking us?" another woman asked as she stepped down from the truck. One of the guards backhanded her and she yelped, falling to the concrete ground.

"Anyone else have a question?" he asked the group. Of course, no one else spoke up. No one dared after the woman was helped up from the floor, holding her jaw, whimpering in pain. The other women were smart enough to keep their mouths shut.

"Good, let's move," another guard shouted. The women

filed into a single line and walked into the warehouse silently. Wherever they were going, Amelia was pretty sure that none of them were going to like their final destination.

They lined up the women in front of cages and she was sure that she had correctly guessed how much she was going to hate what came next. "In," the third guard shouted. Some of the women cried and shook their heads, but Amelia knew that none of that would help save her from the inevitable. She was going to have to get into the disgusting cage behind her, just like all the others.

Amelia stepped into the cage and the guard with kind eyes looked in at her and nodded, as if actually thanking her for her compliance. She shrugged, "No use in fighting," she whispered more to herself than to him. "You do have a gun." She nodded to the semi-automatic he was holding, pointed in her direction.

"Smart girl," the guy drawled, walking over to the next woman in line, and demanding her compliance. She didn't give it as willingly as Amelia had. He forced her into the cage next to Amelia's and she fell to the dirty concrete floor. He shouted at the woman that she needed to learn her place as she scooted across the floor to the back corner of the cage. Amelia wasn't sure how they had all landed in this hell, but she was sure of one thing—it was going to get worse, and as much as she didn't want to admit it, things probably wouldn't get better—ever.

Spider (A Halloween Novella- Royal Bastards MC:

**Huntsville Chapter Book 12) Universal Link->https://
books2read.com/u/38nWA6**

**Did you love Thorne and Rose's story and want to read
more of the Savage Hell MC Series? Here's a peek into
RoadKill, book one of the series!**

SAVAGE
PROLOGUE

SAVAGE SAT IN THE HOLDING CELL, WAITING FOR THE OFFICERS to bring Cillian in to see him. He knew his old friend would call him for help sooner or later. Cillian James was the one he failed, and Savage lived with that disappointment in himself every damn day. Savage was good friends with Cillian's dad and had been since they arrived from Ireland when Cillian was just a kid. He promised to keep an eye on him after his parents went back to Ireland and Cillian stayed in the US, but somewhere along the line, Savage failed him.

When Cillian tried to join Savage's MC, he refused him. Patching in the kid would have been the wrong call. He didn't belong in that group of military misfits and one-percenters who made up his motley crew. To Savage, they were family but to Cillian, they would mean the end of what he wanted—a chance at a normal life. So, he told the kid that he didn't want him and even made up some excuse about him being too hot-tempered for their club, just to throw him off the scent. It had the opposite effect though and Cillian became even more determined to find his way in. Even if that meant joining Savage Hell's rival club—the Dragons. They were bad news and before Savage could step in and save Cillian, he had stolen a car to try to prove his worth to the Dragons. The problem was—they didn't want Cillian and when it came down to it, they let him rot in prison over a gang prank that went wrong.

Their leader thought it would be funny to set Cillian up to take the fall for grand theft auto and he took the bait and was now serving his time for the crime he committed. It pissed Savage off knowing that he could have prevented all of Cillian's problems if he had just let him into Savage Hell. But it was too late to go back and change all of that. All Savage could do now was help his friend and he was hoping that was why he was summoned to the prison so early on a Monday morning.

The steel door creaked open, and Cillian walked in wearing handcuffs and a smile. The officer instructed them that they were not allowed any physical contact, they only had ten minutes for their visit and asked Savage if he wanted Cillian's cuffs on or off.

"Off," Savage growled. As soon as the handcuffs were removed, Cillian sat down on the other side of the table from Savage and nodded.

"Thanks for coming, man," Cillian said.

"No problem, Cillian. It's been a damn long time," Savage

said. "I've been here a few times, but you refused to see me—what was up with that, man?"

Cillian chuckled and Savage sat back to cross his arms over his chest, finding the whole thing less funny than his friend.

"You haven't changed a bit," Cillian said, and Savage just shrugged. "It's been a long time since I heard anyone call me by my real name. I was starting to forget who I was in here."

"Yeah, I heard about all of that," Savage said. "You got into some trouble. I heard you killed a man." Cillian eyed the guard who stood in the corner of the room, watching and listening to every word they were saying.

"Nope," he said. "But I got the credit in the yard for it and that's how I got my nickname—Kill." Cillian flashed Savage a grin and he shook his head.

"It doesn't suit you," Savage growled. "I think I'll stick with your real name, Cillian." His friend didn't seem at all put off by his refusing to use his new nickname, even shrugging it off.

"Suit yourself," he said, his Irish accent sounding in full. Savage didn't realize just how much he had missed his friend until just now.

"It's good to see you," Savage whispered. "So much has happened since you've been in here."

"Yeah well, ten years is a damn long time. And I'm sorry about turning you away when you came to visit but I just couldn't see you. Knowing you were here for me was enough but seeing you would have pained me. I would have longed for a life that I could never have." Cillian's expression was bitter, and Savage realized that the boy he used to know wasn't sitting across the table from him. Cillian had become the man that prison had made him. He truly was 'Kill' now but Savage refused to believe he couldn't have the life he wanted, once he got out of that awful place.

"Why am I here now?" Savage asked, cutting straight to the chase. The guard was watching the clock and he knew that their ten minutes were just about up. It was time to find out why Cillian wanted to see him now after so much time had passed.

"I'm getting out," Cillian breathed.

"That's great, man," Savage said. "When?"

"Probably sometime next week. The date hasn't been set yet, but my lawyer said it's a done deal. I need an advocate on the outside," Cillian all but whispered. "I was hoping it would be you."

"Of course, anything you need, man," Savage offered, and he meant it too.

"I can't be around any felons, as part of my parole conditions," Cillian said. Savage nodded his understanding.

"So, no Savage Hell party at the clubhouse to welcome you home then?" Cillian smiled.

"No," he agreed. "I appreciate the club taking me under its wing after I did what I did with the Dragons. Savage Hell and you have had my back through all of this, but I can't be around most of the guys while I'm on parole."

Savage laughed, "Yeah, they aren't the upstanding citizens your parole officer will want you hanging around with, I'm afraid," he said. "But you have my help—whatever you need."

"Can you pick me up and help me find a place to live and maybe a job, once I get sprung?" Cillian asked. He fidgeted with his own hands on the metal desk and for just a minute, Savage caught a glimpse of the shy boy who came from Ireland and didn't quite fit in anywhere.

"Of course," Savage said. "Consider it done."

"How's the family? I got your letters about Bowie and Dallas—I'm so happy for you, man," Cillian said. Savage wasn't sure if he believed him or not. He could hear the undertones of sadness in Cillian's voice.

"You'll get there too, Cillian. Someday—"

"Don't," Cillian barked. "Don't give me hope for someday, Savage. It hurts too much to think about not having that happiness in my life—a wife, kids—a family. It's not for me now so don't feed me some bullshit about someday," he growled. Savage nodded, knowing that now wasn't the time to argue with his friend. Not when their precious time was ticking down to mere seconds.

"That's time," the guard called. "Let's go, Kill." Cillian stood as ordered and nodded to Savage.

"I'll be here when you get out, Cillian," Savage promised.

"Thanks, man," Cillian said. The guard put the cuffs back on him and he turned to leave the room. "I knew I could count on you, Savage."

CILLIAN

Kɪʟʟ ʜᴀᴅ ʙᴇᴇɴ ᴄᴏᴜɴᴛɪɴɢ ᴅᴏᴡɴ ᴛʜᴇ ᴅᴀʏꜱ ᴛᴏ ʜɪꜱ ʀᴇʟᴇᴀꜱᴇ and what was promised to be only one week away, ended up being two. When the day finally arrived for him to be released, Savage was waiting for him just outside the prison gates as promised. He was the one guy Kill could count on and he had to admit that it felt damn good to have someone on his side for a change.

During his exit interview with his parole officer, he was quickly reminded about the fact that most inmates end up right back in prison after they were let out. Kill didn't want to believe he could so easily end up as a statistic, but it was his biggest fear.

"Hey, man," Savage said, pulling him in for a quick hug. "You look good."

"Yeah, thanks for sending in some clothes for me. The ones they had of mine, from ten years ago, weren't exactly going to fit." Savage looked him up and down as if sizing him up. He was just a kid when he went to prison for grand theft auto—just twenty-three. It seemed like a lifetime ago.

"No," Savage said. "I guess they wouldn't. You have filled out in the last ten years."

Kill laughed, "Yep. Not much else to do in prison besides lift and workout."

"Well, I have a few bags of clothes in the trunk. Nothing fancy, just some stuff the guys got together, and my girl loves to shop. Dallas had a field day picking you up some clothes. She even guessed your size and got you a suit, you know—for job interviews and stuff."

"I appreciate it, Savage. I'll find a way to pay you back," Kill promised.

Savage pointed his finger at Kill. "No, you won't. We're family and family takes care of each other," he said. "Now, get in. We need to get this apartment hunting underway. Until we can find you something, you'll be staying with me and my family. I've already given your parole officer my address and cell number." Savage got into the cab of his black pick-up and Kill slid into the passenger seat. He handed Kill a cell phone and he turned it over in his hand. He had never really had his cell phone and wasn't sure how to work the new ones. He only ever used the ones that flipped open but this one didn't have that feature.

"Push the side button and it turns on. It's charged and I've added you to my family plan," Savage said.

"This is too much, Savage," Kill whispered. It was too. He had forgotten what it meant to have family around and

Savage treating him like a kid brother made him homesick for something that didn't exist anymore.

Kill's parents announced they were moving to the States when he was fourteen. Leaving Ireland felt like he was cutting off one of his appendages. He reluctantly agreed to follow them across the pond, but Ireland was a part of him, and he still longed to go back. But now, he had nothing and no one to go back to. His parents returned home to Ireland just after he turned twenty-one, and he foolishly decided to stay in America. He was trying to get into Savage's MC— Savage Hell and he thought he was too good to go back to his childhood roots. He told his father that he wanted to stay in America and make something of himself, even implying his dad couldn't hack it in the States. God, he was an asshole. His father convinced Savage to keep an eye on him and his parents headed back to Ireland.

About three months later, he got a call from his Mum that his father had died. He had a heart attack in his sleep, and she found him dead the next morning. He didn't even go home for the funeral, even though his mother begged him to. Savage offered to lend him the money, but a mix of pride and being a stubborn ass took over and he refused. It was one of his major regrets and now that he was looking back, probably the one thing that shoved him down the wrong path. His life seemed to spiral out of control after his dad passed and one wrong decision led to the next and before he knew it, Kill was sitting behind the wheel of a stolen car, trying to prove he was worth something.

He begged Savage to let him into Savage Hell. Kill

showed up to the bar that housed the club almost daily and every time Savage denied him; it drove him further over the line. When the Dragons showed interest in him, he jumped at the chance to be a part of a motorcycle club. He thought he'd show Savage just what he was made of by joining the Dragons and then he'd let him into Savage Hell. He was an idiot—he knew that now. But, at the time, it seemed like such a great plan. It wasn't and that point hit home when he realized his new club had set him up. They knew he was mixed up with Savage and they used him to send Savage Hell a message. Dante was the president of the Dragons, and he told Kill that if he wanted to be patched in, he needed to steal a car and bring it to the meeting. He wanted to be a part of something so badly he didn't think through the ramifications and getting caught seemed like a risk worth taking. He didn't even get half a mile down the road with the car he stole before the cops pulled him over. During his hearing, it came out that he was set up by the Dragons who were cooperating fully with the authorities. The judge decided to make an example out of him and gave Kill a twelve-year sentence, of which he served ten and with good behavior, got out.

About a year ago, he got a letter from his aunt in Ireland, telling him that his Mum had passed from cancer. He didn't even know she had the disease, and it just about broke his heart that he didn't get to say goodbye to her. After his sentencing, she wrote him a letter, telling him that she would always love him, but that would be the last he'd ever hear from her, and she was a woman who was true to her word.

"You good, Cillian?" Savage asked.

"Yeah," he lied. "Just thinking about everything. This is all a lot to take in," he admitted.

"Give it time, brother. You will have to do a lot of adjusting, but I believe in you, man. You need help, you use that to call me," Savage ordered, nodding to the cell phone Kill was clutching like it was his lifeline.

"Will do," Kill agreed. "And, thanks, Savage."

"Don't thank me yet, Cillian. You're bunking with the new baby, and he'll keep you up all damn night long." Savage laughed.

"Remember, I've been in prison for the last ten years. Rooming with a newborn will be a piece of cake," Kill said.

"Yeah, we'll see if you're humming the same tune tomorrow morning when he wakes you up at four A.M., man," Savage said. "Welcome to the family, Cillian." Savage had no idea what those words meant to him, and Cillian swallowed past the lump of emotion in his throat. It felt damn good to have a family again—now he just needed to find his place in the world—his home.

VIVIAN

Vivian Ward wasn't sure how she was going to fit in everything on her to-do list today, but she was determined to make that happen, even if it ended up killing her. The diner was once again short-handed, thanks to a teenage employee who thought it was all right to give all her friends free food. Viv knew her grandmother would have given the girl a second chance to, "Make things right," as she liked to say but that wasn't her style. Viv was hardcore when it came to giving people second chances, a life lesson she learned when she found her husband in bed with the town whore.

She had been married to Jason for almost three years when she came home early from her restaurant to surprise him. Truth was, she was the one surprised, to find him in bed with another woman. He made excuses and God help her, she was stupid and desperate enough to believe him. Hell, she even forgave him but that was just part of her need to be wanted and loved—well, according to her therapist. They had done the whole therapy thing and a year later, almost to the day, when she found her husband's secretary on her knees, under his desk giving him a blow job, she was done. Viv walked out of his office and went home to pack up his shit and kicked him the fuck out of her house. Honestly, it was the best decision she had ever made, and she didn't regret leaving Jason even once. Sure, she was a little lonelier, but she would rather be alone and happy then with a man she couldn't trust. Gone were the days when she'd sit at home and worry that her beloved husband was making bad decisions. Every time he couldn't account for his where-abouts, she'd go half-crazy and fly off the handle, only to let his soothing lies calm her. Yeah, she was a class A fool but not anymore. She was done with liars, done with cheaters, and done with men in general. Lesson learned.

Today, she had bigger problems. She was down to just two employees and one of them was a new trainee. She was fucked until she could find another person to hire. Putting an ad in the paper and waiting for the right person to walk through the door took time—time she didn't have.

She blew into the diner like a tornado and found Tina going over how to refill the napkin holders with the new guy —who's name she could never remember—and Viv rolled her eyes. "You know Tina," she said seeming to startle them both, "I'm pretty sure that filling a napkin holder is self-explanatory." Tina nodded and handed the empty napkin holder and a stack of napkins to the trainee and bounced off into the kitchen. Viv suddenly felt way too old to be keeping company with the teens she usually hired. At twenty-eight, she should feel anything but old. But that was the problem with owning the town's only diner. Teens seemed to flock to the place in droves and they were also the ones who usually answered her ads for employment. Maybe if she held out this time, she'd find someone who could not only help wait tables but also have some experience behind the grills. Her current cook showed up to work on the days he was sober and those were becoming few and far between. She needed to get her grandmother's old place back on track and running as smoothly as it had when Gram was alive.

When Viv was seventeen, her Gram dropped the bomb that would forever change Viv's life—she had cancer and not much time left. Gram had raised Viv since her father took off and her mother died. She was only six years old when the two most important people in her life abandoned her, but Gram stuck around. It took time to realize that her grandmother wasn't going anywhere and when Gram announced that she had terminal cancer, it hit Viv hard. She promised her Gram that she would take care of her beloved diner but that was easier said than done. Her grandmother fought hard but when Viv was twenty, she passed, leaving her to take care of everything—alone. She had never felt so lonely, not even after divorcing Jason. Her grandmother was her everything. Maybe that was why she was willing to overlook all of Jason's flaws and accept his marriage proposal. Viv believed that being with someone—anyone—was better than being alone. But boy, was she wrong.

Luckily for her, Gram had taught Viv the ropes at a very young age. She had been helping in the diner her whole life and taking over ownership of the place wasn't a stretch for her. Her grandmother had thought of everything and arranged for her lawyers to handle the transfer upon her death. Viv showed up to work the day after the funeral and opened the doors for business, much as she always had. It's what her grandmother wanted, and she honored her wishes. Gram insisted that she get on with her life as quickly as possible and Viv promised to try. Throwing herself back into her work seemed as good a way as any to get on with life.

"Hey, new guy," she shouted. The trainee turned from trying to shove way too many napkins into the holder and pointed to himself as if to ask, "Me?". Viv sighed and nodded. "Do you see any other new guys around?" she asked. Sure, she sounded like a class-A bitch, but she didn't care.

"N-no," he stuttered.

"You wait tables on your own yet?" she asked but Viv already knew the answer by his blank stare. "All right then," she said under her breath. "Today you learn to wait tables on your own. It's sink or swim time, New Guy," she said.

"Um, my name is Tommy," he nervously offered.

"Of course, it is," she whispered to herself. "Okay, Tommy," she said, turning to hand him an order pad and pencil. "You write everything down. If someone says to hold the onions, write the letter O down next to the order and then cross it out," she said. Tommy nodded and started jotting down notes as she went over everything and she couldn't help her smile at remembering the way Gram used to ride her for not using the correct codes for the kitchen.

Viv had taken to abbreviating everything and when her order went back to the cook, he had no freaking idea what the hell to make of it. Gram told her to get it straight or she'd have to deal with the pissed-off kitchen staff. After she was yelled at a few times by the cook, Viv learned quickly to avoid his temper and write the correct fucking codes down on her order pad.

"Get the codes right or deal with the cook," she barked at Tommy. He nodded and started to write down her orders, word for word, and she sighed again. "This is going to be a long fucking day," she breathed.

Viv busied herself getting the diner ready to open and didn't even see the wall of man that she ran into while making her way to the back storeroom. "What the fuck?" Viv growled, taking a step back to get her bearings. The guy's big, tattoo-covered hands quickly reached out to her, helping her to find her balance.

"Who are you and how the fuck did you get in here before we're open?" Viv asked. She looked him up and down and realized that most of his exposed skin was covered in ink and she had to admit, it was hot. She had always liked bad boys even if she had married a clean-cut accountant the first time around. Her grandmother used to say, "If he rides a motorcycle or has tattoos, my granddaughter will date him." She wondered what her Gram would think of the sexy man standing in front of her now. His light brown hair was long and wavy, hanging down to his broad shoulders. Honestly, he had better hair than she did, and she was suddenly regretting her decision to go a third day without washing it, opting for a messy bun. He looked like he worked out but not the way the muscle heads at the gym did. This guy looked more naturally fit but his muscles seemed to have muscles. His amused smirk told her he wasn't buying her tough girl routine either.

"I'm here for breakfast," he said, and his voice sounded like a warm brandy coating her soul.

"You're not from around here, are you?" Viv asked.

He chuckled, "Nope," he said. "Although I call the fair state of Alabama my home now, I'm originally from Ireland."

Dear Lord, Viv felt about ready to burst into flames just from his sexy voice alone. His accent made it harder for her to concentrate on what her next question or comment should be. Hell, she was pretty sure that remembering her name might be a task.

"Can I get some food?" he asked when she didn't respond.

"Food?" she repeated as though she didn't understand the word.

"Sure—you know, stuff you eat. Listen, I have a busy day and I just need to fuel up." Viv looked down at her watch and back up at the sexy, tatted man before her. He took off his black leather jacket and flung it over his shoulder, giving her a better look at not only his tattoos but his muscles. And holy arm porn—he was hot!

"Fine," she said, trying for a little pissed off but sounding a whole lot more turned on. Shit!

"I'll just sit here at the counter if that works," he offered. She didn't say a word, not sure that anything she uttered would make any sense. Viv just stood there nodding like a fool and watched as he walked past her to find a stool at the front counter. She nearly swallowed her tongue at how good his ass looked in the black jeans that hugged him like a glove. She shook her head as if trying to regain her senses.

"New guy," she barked. "You're up."

"Tommy," he called from the corner of the diner. "My name is Tommy," he complained.

"Yeah, yeah. Tommy—you're up," Viv corrected and didn't miss the way hot biker guy laughed.

"Keep laughing," she warned. "Tommy here is in training and you're his first real customer," she said not hiding her smile. "Good luck to you, Sir," she said and turned to finish her work in the back storeroom. She needed to take a quick inventory for the day, especially since her now ex-employee fed her friends as though it was her personal pantry. She'd call in her order and then find the time to post a new ad in the local paper.

By the time she finished her inventory, New Guy had not only brought Hot Irish Guy his food, but they were chatting it up like they were old friends. "Don't you have something you could be doing?" Viv looked Tommy up and down and took a sadistic pleasure in the way he hopped out of her way and pretended to be busy.

"Sure, boss," he said. Viv pulled the sugar shakers from

the counter underneath the bar and started to refill them. "Oh, Tina said to tell you she had to leave for the day. Something about a family emergency," Tommy said. He shot her a look that suggested he should be afraid to deliver the message and New Guy was right. She felt about ready to lob a sugar shaker at his head but that would only involve paperwork and workman's comp claims she didn't have time for.

"Great," she mumbled. "That girl has more family emergencies than anyone else I've ever met. Just how big is her family anyway?" Viv complained to herself.

Hot Irish guy seemed to find her whole monologue funny. "So, your employees giving you trouble?" he questioned. He shoved four pieces of bacon and half a piece of toast into his mouth.

"Trouble doesn't begin to describe what they are causing me today—or any other day, for that matter," she admitted. "I just fired Tina's best friend for feeding half the town for free and now she takes off with her same old tired excuse. It's just me and the New Kid," she said, nodding to where Tommy was still fumbling with the napkin dispensers.

Hot Irish guy cleared his throat, "I might be able to help with your troubles," he said. God, Viv thought of about a thousand ways that man could help with her problems, and not one of them involved what he was probably about to propose. "Hire me," he said, holding his arms wide as if he was making a sacrifice to her.

"What are your qualifications, Hot Irish Guy?" she asked.

"Hot Irish Guy?" He questioned her nickname for him.

Honestly, she was awful at names, so she usually made up her own for people.

Viv shrugged, "Well, it's accurate," she said. She put down the sugar shaker she was working on and studied him. "Really, why would you want to work here? I usually get high schoolers coming in here to ask me for a job, but you look to be well out of the public school system."

He threw back his head and barked out his laugh and it was probably the sexiest thing Viv had ever seen in her life. "Yeah, I'm well past school age, Darlin'," he admitted. "I've just turned thirty-three." Now it was Viv's turn to laugh. He sounded as though he was saying "tirty-tree".

"Yeah, yeah—go ahead and make fun of the way I say my th's; everyone does." He shot her a sexy smirk that had Viv immediately stop laughing. This guy seemed to be able to take the whole smolder thing to a whole new level.

"My question stands," she said. "Why do you want to work here?"

He shrugged and pushed his empty plate to the back of the counter, leaning forward as if he was about to share a secret with her. Viv did the same, eager to share the same space as the sexy guy. "I'm a felon," he loudly whispered.

She didn't even blink an eye. She had known a few ex-cons in her life. Her grandmother even dated one for a few years until he got bored and took off. So, Hot Irish Guy's grand admission didn't shock her. "And incapable of whispering," Viv teased.

"You don't seem surprised." He sounded almost disappointed in the fact that he didn't surprise her.

"Let's just say that my grandmother sometimes ran with a questionable crowd, and I've known all kinds," she said. "So, you want a job here because you're a felon? You look other places?" Viv knew she was sticking her nose into a stranger's business, but she couldn't help herself. Plus, if he wanted her to consider him for employment, she had a right to ask questions. Although, she was pretty sure that the question she wanted to ask was completely inappropriate. His relationship status didn't factor into whether she would hire him or not.

"Yeah," he admitted. "I've put into just about every place on Main Street that's hiring and nothing. I have to fill out their applications and when I get to the part where I have to answer 'yes' for convicted of a felony, it's over. No one wants to hire an ex-con." Viv hated that he seemed almost defeated and whether right or wrong, she wanted to help him.

"What did you do?" she asked.

"Grand theft auto," he answered. "I was a stupid kid—just trying to get into a motorcycle gang. My family had just gone back to Ireland and left me in America, and I didn't exactly fit in." Viv giggled at the thought of an Irish kid trying to fit in with the kids around town. Kids in their little Alabama town were tough when it came to accepting anyone new into the fold. Given the fact that he sounded so different from them, Hot Irish Guy might have never found his place.

"I got about eight hundred meters before the cops caught up to me. I found out later that the guys in the gang I was trying to join set me up. I was made an example of by the system and served ten years of a twelve-year sentence."

"Wow, that's awful," Viv said, and she meant it. What happened to him sucked and not giving him a chance to turn himself around would be a dishonor to her Gram. He was just the type of person her grandmother was constantly trying to help. And now it was Viv's turn to lend a hand. Of course, it didn't hurt that Hot Irish Guy was—well, hot.

"I have two questions," Viv said.

"Shoot," he said, leaning back in his stool.

"Can you cook and when can you start?" His smile almost lit up the place and she knew she did the right thing even if New Kid was shooting her daggers from the back of the diner.

"What's the problem, New Kid?" she asked.

"He's not going to outrank me, right?" he asked.

"I don't think that's even possible, New Kid," Viv said, rolling her eyes for good measure. "Now back to work and stop eavesdropping." She watched as Tommy pretended to wipe down the booth that he had been working on for the past ten minutes.

"How about we take this to my office, and you can fill out the paperwork?" Hot Irish Guy nodded and grabbed his dishes.

"Thank you," he said, following her back through the kitchen to deposit his dishes into the sink. He followed her back to her tiny office and crammed into her space, making it feel even smaller.

"Um—" she squeaked, suddenly feeling nervous. "I guess you should tell me your name—unless you're good with Hot Irish Guy."

He chuckled and his deep baritone laugh filled her office. "It's Cillian James but everyone calls me Kill," he said.

"Kill?" Viv questioned. "That's a pretty ominous name. You have anything else you need to tell me before we make this official?" She asked.

"Nope," he said, taking the papers from her. "I'm good."

CILLIAN

Kɪʟʟ ᴡᴀᴛᴄʜᴇᴅ ᴛʜᴇ ꜱᴇxʏ ʟɪᴛᴛʟᴇ ʙʀᴜɴᴇᴛᴛᴇ ꜰɪᴅɢᴇᴛ ᴀʀᴏᴜɴᴅ her office as if she was too afraid to leave him alone in her space. He didn't blame her. There were a lot of people who didn't trust him, and he'd just add her to that very long list.

He finished filling out the paperwork and realized he didn't know his new boss' name. "Sorry," he said, startling her from her work. "I don't know your name."

"I'm Vivian Ward," she offered. "Usually, the kids who work for me just call me boss, but you can call me Viv." He stood and held out his hand and she hesitantly took it.

"It's good to meet you, Viv," he said. "You won't be sorry you gave me a chance here."

"I don't know." Kill worried that she had already changed her mind and he set the papers down on her desk. "With a nickname like 'Kill', I think I might have bitten off more than

I can chew." The thought of his hot new boss biting anywhere on his body flashed through his mind. He needed to remind his unruly cock that wasn't going to happen—not with her now that he was her employee. At least, he hoped he was still employed.

"Listen, if you're having second thoughts, I understand," he lied. He didn't understand any of what he had been put through this past week since getting out of prison. He had been treated like shit and all he was asking for was a chance to prove that he wasn't that same stupid kid who desperately wanted to be a part of something.

"How about you tell me how you got your nickname and I'll reserve my final decision until you are done sharing your story?" He hated having to recap any of his time in prison but if that was the only way he was going to get a job, he'd do it. Still, it felt wrong to tell someone who seemed as innocent as Vivian Ward about something so personal and dirty from his past.

"I got it from my cellmate, in prison," he whispered. "I was thrown into general population, and I had to survive."

Viv gasped and covered her mouth with her shaking hand. He almost regretted telling her anything. "And you had to kill someone to stay alive?" she guessed.

"Yes, and no," he admitted. "I didn't kill anyone, but everyone believed that I had, so I let them think the worst of me."

"Why would you let them believe you killed a man?" Viv asked. He didn't expect her to understand. Prison changed a person and when you were in there, you learned to do whatever it took to make it out alive.

"We were in the yard—you know having some free time and I was approached by a man they called Capone who was in charge, so to speak, of the prisoners. He had ties to the mafia and was from a rival club on the outside. Even though I had been thrown in prison before becoming a member of the Dragons, he considered me an enemy."

"Why didn't you tell anyone?" she asked. He chuckled at the idea of telling someone what was going on in that yard. Hell, he'd be labeled a snitch and they got a hell of a lot more than stitches in that prison. They ended up in the infirmary if they were lucky and, in the morgue, if they weren't.

"Who was I to tell? If I reported every illegal activity going on in that place to the warden, I'd end up in the morgue. I tried to talk to some of the gang members—you know the ones who set me up? Like my new friend, Capone, they didn't consider me to be a part of their club. They had heard what happened to me on the outside and told me I was on my own."

"What happened next?" Viv asked. She sat in front of him, on the edge of her desk and it took all his restraint not to reach out and pull her onto his lap. Feck, she was sexy, and he was going to have to work damn hard to remind himself that she was off-limits. He had to admit the way she seemed to take an interest in him turned him inside out. It had been over ten years since he was with a woman. Hell, he'd been out for a week and the first thing he wanted to do was find a willing woman and spend a night losing himself in her, but he didn't. That would have been his way of falling back into his old habits and he couldn't let that happen. It was the straight and narrow for him and that meant no gangs, no drugs, and no hookers, no matter how much his dick screamed for attention.

"When Capone heard that I was on my own, left for dead by my own supposed club, he did something that completely surprised me—asked me to join his prison club. I had nothing to lose and everything to gain by taking him up on his offer. When the rival gang came after him for taking me in, a guy got killed. Capone was the one who shanked him but gave me the credit. He knew that with a rumor like that going around, that I killed a guy, I'd be safe while serving my time. Capone took the blame and had time added onto his sentence and I got the nickname 'Kill'," he said.

"Wow," she breathed.

"Wow is an understatement," he admitted. "Hell, if I hadn't taken his offer, I'd be dead now. He taught me the ropes and kept me safe," Kill said. He thought about his friend still sitting in that prison and felt an unexplainable sadness that he had gotten out.

"Aw—a bad guy with a heart of gold," Viv said, interrupting his thoughts.

"Yeah, you could say that about a lot of the guys on the inside. I know this might sound crazy but I'm going to miss that camaraderie," he admitted. As soon as he got out, he met with his probation officer who informed him that meeting with any type of club or gang would land him back in prison and he would do anything not to have that happen.

"Why can't you join a club out here?" Viv asked.

"It goes against my parole. It would be considered a violation since trying to join a motorcycle club was what landed me behind bars, to begin with," he said.

"Oh, I'm sorry." She reached out and placed her small hand over his forearm and his skin felt strange—almost like pins and needles. Yeah, he was going to have to find a woman and let off some steam if just a simple touch from his new boss set his skin tingling.

He pulled his arm free from her hand and pretended to stretch to cover his retreat. "No," he said. "It's just a part of what I have to do to stay on the outside— you know, find a job and a place to live and keep my nose clean."

"How long have you been out?" she asked.

"About a week," he whispered.

"Do you have everything you need?" Viv looked him up and down and damn if she didn't look just as turned on as he felt. She cleared her throat, "I mean, did you find a place to live and all that?"

"I'm working on the job part first and staying in a motel that's a shit hole, but the owner lets me rent by the week. I figure getting a job trumps a place to live if I can't pay the rent. My friend said I could bunk at his place, but he's got a family and a new kid. The last thing he needed was an ex-con hanging around. After a few nights with his family, I felt like a nuisance. I made some apologies and came up with an excuse as to why I had to leave. It was just too much for me— going from a small prison cell with one roommate to a house full of people. I think Savage understood. At least, I hope he's not pissed that I turned down his generosity and opted for my shithole apartment."

Viv nodded. "You have a friend named Savage?" she asked.

Kill smiled at the fact that little piece of information was her takeaway. "Yeah," he breathed.

"Well, um—you have a job," she said. "As long as you're okay with me calling you by your given name, Cillian. And if you need a better place to stay, I have a house about a block away. It was my grandmother's." She paused, "All of this was hers and she left it to me."

"I'm fine with you calling me whatever you'd like. Hot Irish Guy, Kill or Cillian—as long as I have a job," he said. "And I'm sorry about your grandmother. Losing family sucks," Kill said.

"It's fine. She's been gone awhile now but I think she would have liked you. She always routed for an underdog, and you seem to be as down on your luck as they come. How about you move into my spare room? We can work out the details of pay and I can take your rent out of that." He wasn't sure what to make of her kind offer. On the one hand, he needed a place to stay long term and he had to admit that any place had to be better than the motel he was currently in. But his gut was telling him that living under the same roof as his sexy new boss was a giant mistake. The last time his gut screamed at him that way was the night he decided to do the stupidest thing in his life and steal a car.

He ignored his gut and nodded. "Thanks, Viv," he said. "I'll take you up on your offer of the room and I can start now if you need." He pointed back to where he remembered the kitchen to be located.

"Great," she said. "You never answered my other question, you know."

He thought back over their conversation, trying to pinpoint which question she was talking about. "Oh?"

"Yeah, the one about you having any cooking experience," she reminded.

"It just so happens that you're in luck, Darlin'," he said. "I was put on kitchen duty while in the clink and I learned from the best fry cook you'll ever meet." Viv's smile brightened up her tiny office.

"Perfect," she beamed. "Let's get you started." She stood and led the way out of her office and all Kill seemed capable of doing was watching her sexy little ass sashay out. Yeah—he should have listened to his gut when it came to his hot as fuck new boss. He was a glutton for a punishment and Kill was pretty sure that having to live under the same roof as Viv, and keeping his hands to himself, was going to be a pretty big fucking punishment to endure.

Don't miss the other books in the Savage Hell MC series! These titles are available NOW!

RoadKill-> https://books2read.com/u/bWPeRM

REPOssession->https://books2read.com/u/bMXDa5

Dirty Ryder->https://books2read.com/u/3RnyxR

Hart's Desire-> https://books2read.com/u/bpzJ9k

Axel's Grind-> https://books2read.com/u/3Gw9oK

Razor's Edge-> https://books2read.com/u/m0lepY

Trista's Truth-> https://books2read.com/u/med5Rr

Thorne's Rose-> https://books2read.com/u/4jND2l

ABOUT K.L. RAMSEY & BE KELLY

Romance Rebel fighting for Happily Ever After!

K. L. Ramsey currently resides in West Virginia (Go Mountaineers!). In her spare time, she likes to read romance novels, go to WVU football games and attend book club (aka-drink wine) with girlfriends. K. L. enjoys writing Contemporary Romance, Erotic Romance, and Sexy Ménage! She loves to write strong, capable women and bossy, hot as hell alphas, who fall ass over tea kettle for them. And of course, her stories always have a happy ending. But wait—there's more!

Somewhere along the writing path, K.L. developed a love of ALL things paranormal (but has a special affinity for shifters <YUM!!>)!! She decided to take a chance and create another persona- BE Kelly- to bring you all of her yummy shifters, seers, and everything paranormal (plus a hefty dash of MC!).

K. L. RAMSEY'S SOCIAL MEDIA

Ramsey's Rebels - K.L. Ramsey's Readers Group
https://www.facebook.com/groups/ramseysrebels

KL Ramsey & BE Kelly's ARC Team
https://www.facebook.com/
groups/klramseyandbekellyarcteam

KL Ramsey and BE Kelly's Newsletter
https://mailchi.mp/4e73ed1b04b9/authorklramsey/

KL Ramsey and BE Kelly's Website
https://www.klramsey.com

f facebook.com/kl.ramsey.58
instagram.com/itsprivate2
BB bookbub.com/profile/k-l-ramsey
twitter.com/KLRamsey5
a amazon.com/K.L.-Ramsey/e/B0799P6JGJ

BE KELLY'S SOCIAL MEDIA

BE Kelly's Reader's group
https://www.facebook.com/
groups/kellsangelsreadersgroup/

WORKS BY K. L. RAMSEY

The Relinquished Series Box Set

Love Times Infinity

Love's Patient Journey

Love's Design

Love's Promise

Harvest Ridge Series Box Set

Worth the Wait

The Christmas Wedding

Line of Fire

Torn Devotion

Fighting for Justice

Last First Kiss Series Box Set

Theirs to Keep

Theirs to Love

Theirs to Have

Theirs to Take

Second Chance Summer Series

True North

The Wrong Mister Right

Royal Bastards MC

Savage Heat

Whiskey Tango

Can't Fix Cupid

Ratchet's Revenge

Patched for Christmas

Love at First Fight

Dizzy's Desire

Possessing Demon

Mistletoe and Mayhem

Bullseye- Struck by Cupid's Arrow

Legend

Spider

Savage Hell MC Series

Roadkill

REPOssession

Dirty Ryder

Hart's Desire

Axel's Grind

Razor's Edge

Trista's Truth

Thorne's Rose

Lone Star Rangers

Don't Mess With Texas

Sweet Adeline

Dash of Regret

Austin's Starlet

Ranger's Revenge

Heart of Stone

Smokey Bandits MC Series

Aces Wild

Queen of Hearts

Full House

King of Clubs

Joker's Wild

Betting on Blaze

Tirana Brothers (Social Rejects Syndicate

Llir

Altin

Veton

Tirana Brothers Boxset

Dirty Desire Series

Torrid

Clean Sweep

No Limits

Mountain Men Mercenary Series

Eagle Eye

Hacker

Widowmaker

Deadly Sins Syndicate (Mafia Series)

Pride

Envy

Greed

Lust

Wrath

Sloth

Gluttony

Deadly Sins Syndicate Boxset

Forgiven Series

Confession of a Sinner

Confessions of a Saint

Confessions of a Rebel

Chasing Serendipity Series

Kismet

Sealed With a Kiss Series

Kissable

Never Been Kissed

Garo Syndicate Trilogy

Edon

Bekim

Rovena

Garo Syndicate Boxset

Billionaire Boys Club

His Naughty Assistant

His Virgin Assistant

His Nerdy Assistant

His Curvy Assistant

His Bossy Assistant

His Rebellious Assistant

Grumpy Mountain Men Series

Grizz

Jed

Axel

A Grumpy Mountain Man for Xmas

The Bridezilla Series

Happily Ever After- Almost

Picture Perfect

Haunted Honeymoon for One

Rope 'Em and Ride 'Em Series

Saddle Up

A Cowboy for Christmas

Summer Lovin' Series

Beach Rules

Making Waves

Endless Summer

The Bound Series

Bound by Her Mafia Bosses

Bound by His Mafia Princess

Dirty Riders MC Series

Riding Hard

Riding Dirty

Riding Steel

The Dirty Daddies Series

Doctor Daddy

Baby Daddy

A Princess for Daddy

A Daddy for Christmas

The Kink Club Series

Salacious

Insatiable

WORKS BY BE KELLY (K.L.'S ALTER EGO…)

Reckoning MC Seer Series

Reaper

Tank

Raven

Reckoning MC Series Box Set

Perdition MC Shifter Series

Ringer

Rios

Trace

Perdition 3 Book Box Set

Silver Wolf Shifter Series

Daddy Wolf's Little Seer

Daddy Wolf's Little Captive

Daddy Wolf's Little Star

Rogue Enforcers

Juno

Blaze

Elite Enforcers

A Very Rogue Christmas Novella

One Rogue Turn

Graystone Academy Series

Eden's Playground

Violet's Surrender

Holly's Hope (A Christmas Novella)

Renegades Shifter Series

Pandora's Promise

Kinsley's Pact

Leader of the Pack Series

Wren's Pack

Printed in Great Britain
by Amazon

28282285R00089